BLOBBIFS!
SEARCH FOR THE GOLDEN HEART

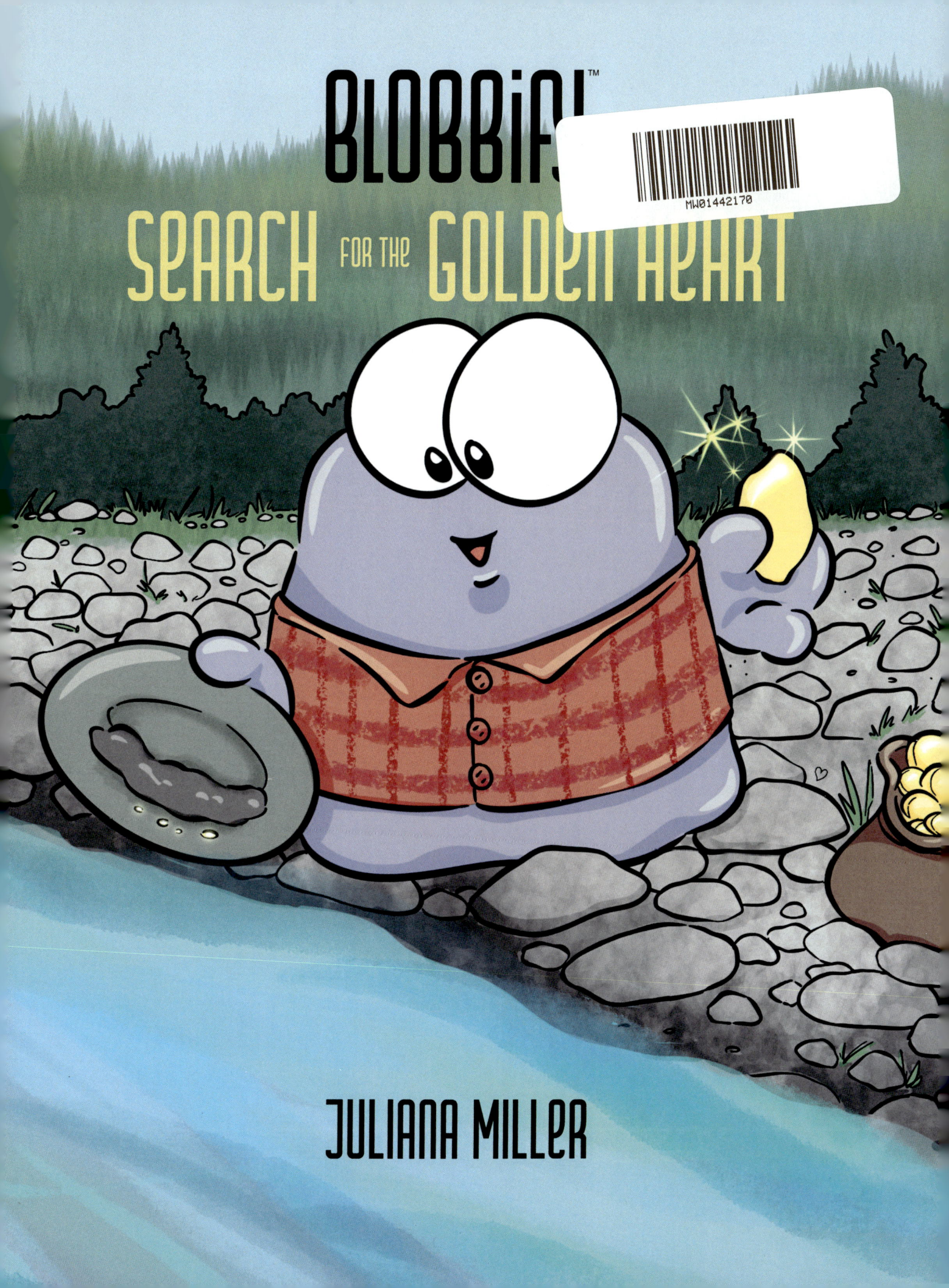

JULIANA MILLER

BLOBBIFY™

Copyright © 2023 Juliana Miller

Blobbify and its characters are the intellectual property of Juliana Miller. All Rights Reserved. No part of this publication may be reproduced, distributed, or transmitted in any form or by any means, including photocopying, recording, or other electronic or mechanical methods, without the prior written permission of the publisher, except in the case of brief quotations embodied in critical reviews and certain other noncommercial uses permitted by copyright law. For permission requests, contact Juliana Miller, PO Box 55742, North Pole, AK 99705.

ISBN 9798390559062

Independently published.

This book has been the most ambitious project I have completed so far. While it has been challenging, it's been rewarding. A heartfelt thanks to all of the businesses and destinations who "got it" and caught the vision. Without your foresight this project would not have been possible.

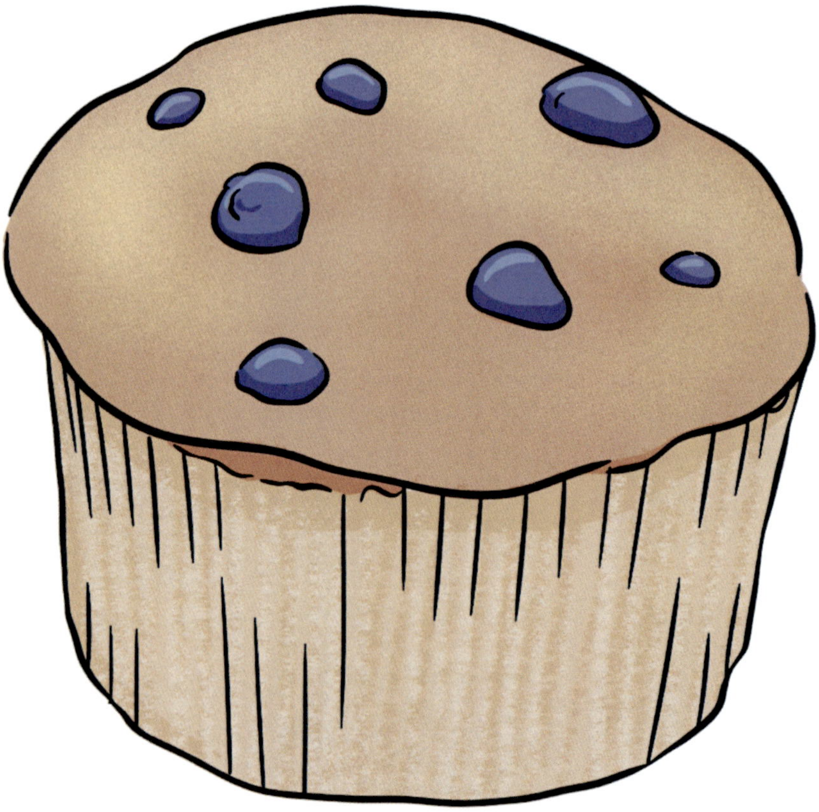

Blobby sat at the kitchen table eating breakfast, devouring his mother Brenda's famous freshly baked blueberry muffins. It was his last day of school before summer break. To add to his excitement, Blobby was expecting a letter from his dear friend Blobbette Butterfield, who had recently moved away from their small town of Blobbington.

When the day was over, Blobby stepped off the school bus and raced toward his mom, who was quietly waiting for him outside. In her hands was a colorful postcard from Blobbette!

Blobby turned the postcard over a few times, admiring the bright blue skies and the gushing fountain in the photo.

He read the message his best friend had written.

FROM: Blobbette B.
PO Box 55742
North Pole, AK
99705

TO: Blobby R.
1259 Goo Lane
Blobbington, MO
59101

Hi Blobby!
I miss you! We are doing well, but I wish you could come visit Alaska! Fairbanks is called the Golden Heart City. It makes me think of you!
♡ Blobbette

A City with a Golden Heart? Blobby was intrigued. He pulled out his history book and reviewed the section he remembered seeing about the Klondike Gold Rush of the early 1900s.

When gold was discovered there, many prospectors had rushed to the interior of Alaska. A trading post was quickly established on the banks of the Chena River. The population near the trading post grew, and the city of Fairbanks was born.

Before he knew it, Blobby was daydreaming of panning for gold and imagining how much a shiny heart made of gold might weigh.

Blobby made his way to his mom and flipped to the section about gold and the adventures of the early pioneers.

His mom grinned and pulled out two small slips of paper. "Would you enjoy your own adventure in Alaska?"

Blobby nodded slowly, his jaw hanging open in stunned silence.

His mom laughed softly. "I have been planning a trip to visit the Butterfields."

Blobby wiggled and hummed as he packed his suitcase. He squeezed the well-loved stuffy his mom had made for him, inhaling the comforting smell of home. "Let's find some gold, Bubby!" he squealed before placing him in his backpack.

The flight to Fairbanks was Blobby's first time on an airplane. At first, there wasn't much to see, but it didn't stop him from peering out the window every few minutes. Whenever turbulence jostled them, his mom squeezed his hand softly.

The plane was a buzz of exhilarated chatter as the blobs began their descent into the Tanana Valley. They flew into Fairbanks, but the Tanana Valley held other smaller communities Blobby hoped they could visit.

He overheard the blobs behind him discussing their plans to visit Santa Claus in North Pole. "Is there really a town called North Pole, Mom?" Blobby asked.

"There sure is," she said as she pulled his backpack out from under their seats. "We are staying at a place in the city of North Pole!"

Arrivals

As they exited the airport, Blobby spotted Blobbette's familiar face. She waited for him with her mother, Brooke. He nearly dropped his backpack when he bolted to her. He squished her with the biggest hug he could give.

"I missed you," his best friend said.

The blobs loaded up their suitcases and drove toward the highway.

Blobbette pointed out the shining Aurora Archway as they passed beneath it. Blobby marveled at the colors that reflected from the sculpture's surface.

He had never seen the aurora borealis, but he imagined this sculpture was appropriately named.

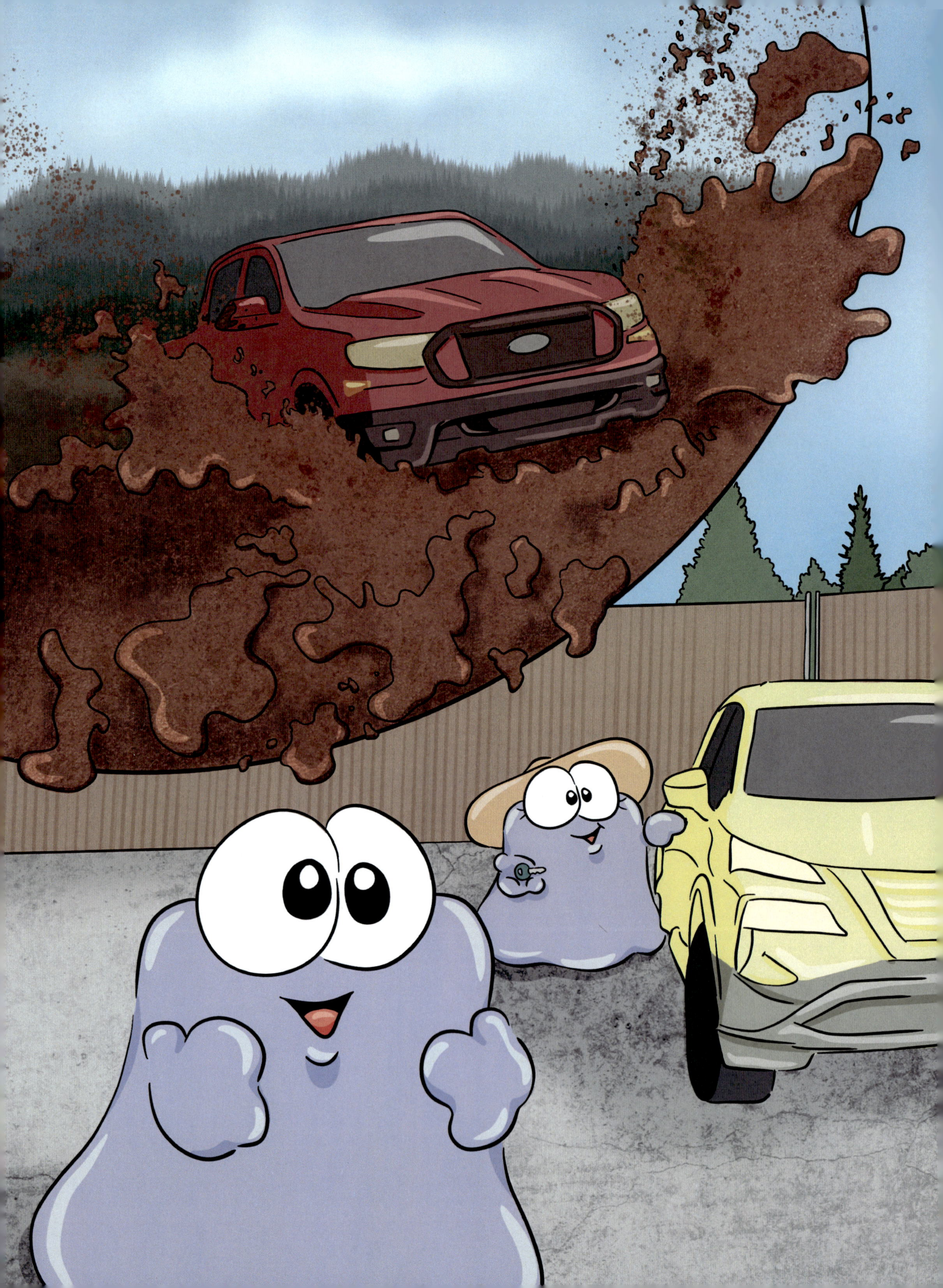

When they arrived at Alaska Auto Rental, his mom got the keys to their car. She loaded their suitcases while Blobby imagined the places they could go. Her laughter tore him from his daydream. "Blobby, we are not here to go off-roading across Alaska."

Blobby waved goodbye to Blobbette as they drove away. "You guys settle into your rental. We'll see you later today!" Brooke called out as they drove away.

Yawning, Blobby sat back in his seat as they began the twenty minute drive to North Pole. His mom had reserved a lakeside Christmas-themed bed-and-breakfast. As they unloaded their suitcases, Blobby bounced and pointed to the blobs who were drifting across the lake in a canoe. They serenely paddled along as he pulled his suitcase into their rental.

WELCOME
NORTH POLE
LAKESIDE
CABINS
ALASKA
AUTO RENTAL
907-457-7368

Soon they ventured out to explore downtown Fairbanks. It was nothing like Blobby had imagined. He thought it would appear more like the pictures from the Gold Rush and pioneer times.

"Don't worry, Blobby," his mom said softly as they walked into River City Café. "After this, we'll be seeing Blobbette and her mom. I think they're bringing along their youngest blob, Billy. They're meeting us at a park that has some of the first cabins built in Fairbanks."

As they went to the counter to make their order, Blobby wondered if they could go inside the old cabins. He got a strawberry Italian soda and a blueberry scone, and his mom got an iced coffee to sip on and big bag of Kaladi Brother's Coffee to take home to Blobbington.

PIONEER PARK

After a refreshing date at the café, Blobby was energized. They entered Pioneer Park, and right as they walked through the entrance, a train rattled overhead. The noise of the shrill whistle startled him, but he was quickly distracted by the many joyful blobs who waved and shouted hello from above.

They discovered Blobbette and Billy at one of the playgrounds. They wandered through the old pioneer town, and Blobby was thrilled that they did get to go inside the old cabins.

The logs were aged and cracked, but still stood strong. His favorite was the cabin selling ice cream.

On their way home, Blobby realized how hungry he had become. He and Blobbette had spent most of their time at the playground, pretending to prospect for gold. The ice cream had held him over for a bit, but his stomach was now rumbling like a thunderstorm. They stopped for dinner at Little Richard's Family Diner, a place famous for its breakfast, burgers, and frosty milkshakes.

He devoured the best burger and fries he had ever eaten. The meat was perfectly cooked, with just the right amount of sear on the outside and oh so juicy on the inside. The fries were crisp on the outside and fluffy on the inside. He slurped down a delicious milkshake. He chose his favorite flavor—cookies and cream!

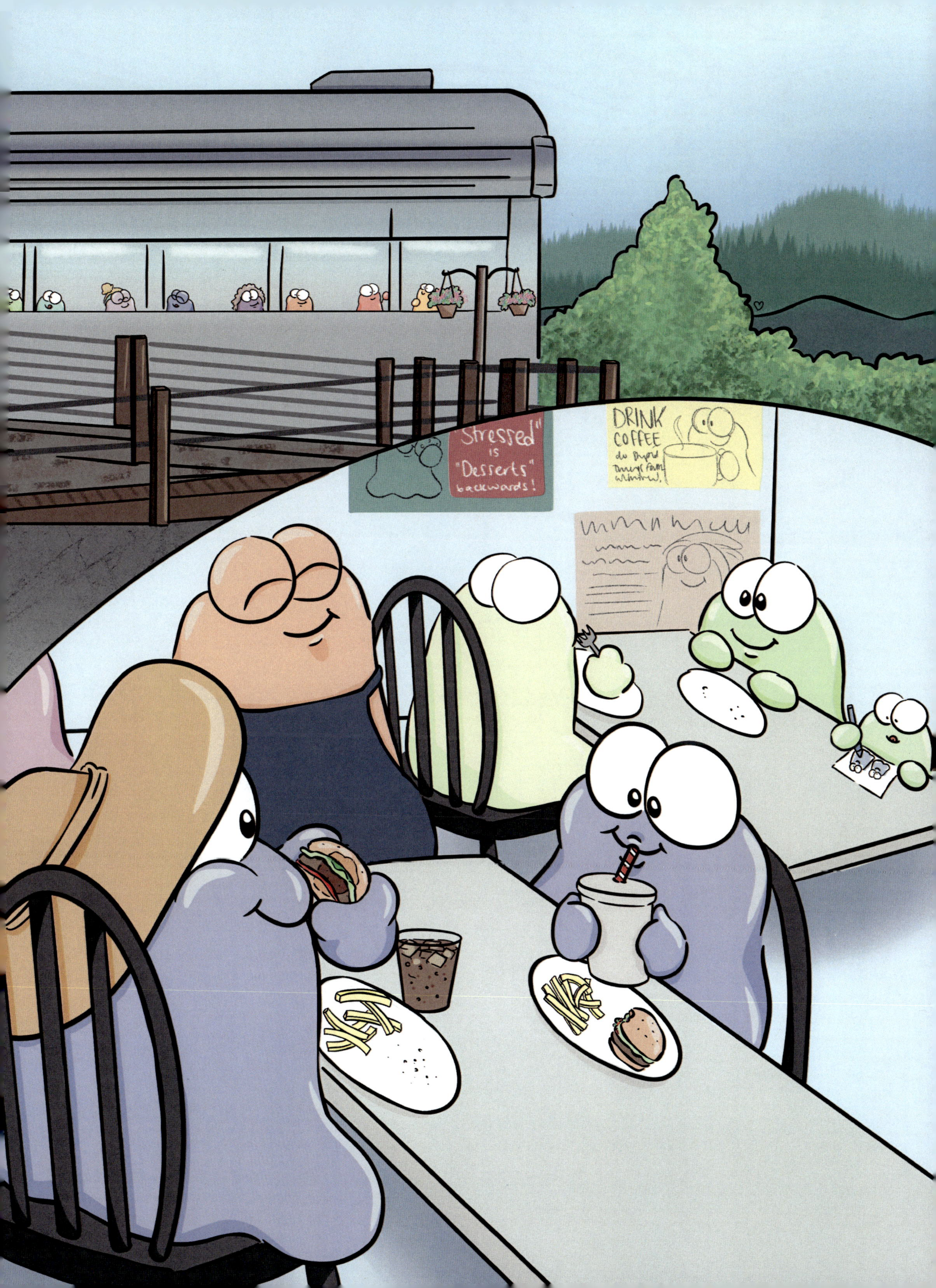
"Stressed"
is
"Desserts"
backwards!
DRINK
COFFEE

As they neared their bed-and-breakfast, Blobby saw something amazing.

He had heard Santa lived at the North Pole, and now he knew it was true. Right in front of him was his house, with an enormous Santa and a sign nearby that read "SANTA CLAUS HOUSE"!

Blobby gazed up at the large, decorated tree as they went inside. He fidgeted and barely spoke as he got his picture with Santa. He was busy absorbing the wonders that surrounded him.

As they left Santa's house, Blobby spotted a fenced park with real reindeer. He enjoyed watching them shuffle around eating grass. He giggled to himself—he had almost forgotten it was still summer. He saw Santa, reindeer, and a big Christmas tree, and to top it off, the light poles throughout the city were specially painted like candy canes.

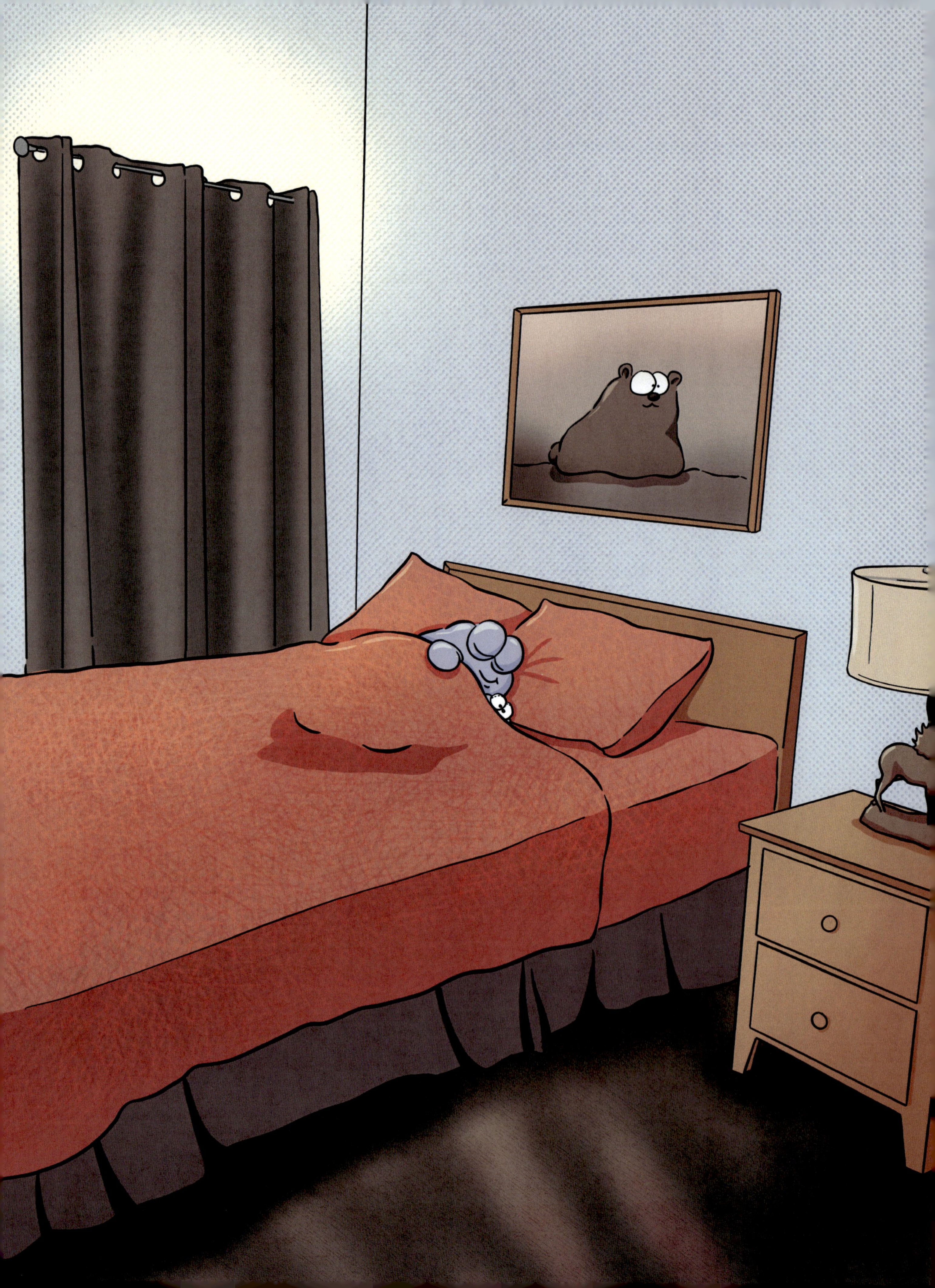

Blobby finally understood why the Tanana Valley was called the land of the midnight sun. Due to how far north they were, the sun shone all through the night during summer. Moments after he melted into his soft bed, he was asleep. He was so tired he wasn't bothered by the golden sunlight peeking through the curtains.

The next morning, Blobby and Brenda met Blobbette and Brooke for breakfast at LuLu's Bread and Bagels.

PLEASE DO NOT FEED THE BAKERS

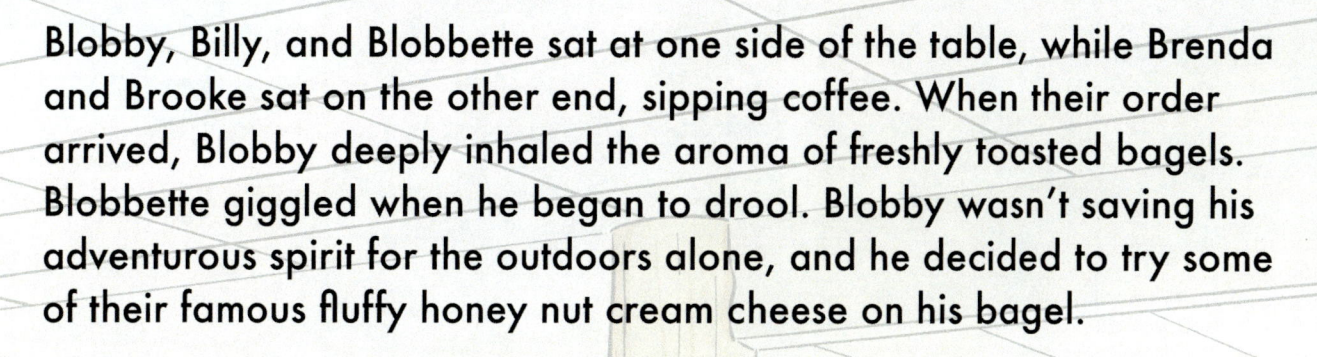

Blobby, Billy, and Blobbette sat at one side of the table, while Brenda and Brooke sat on the other end, sipping coffee. When their order arrived, Blobby deeply inhaled the aroma of freshly toasted bagels. Blobbette giggled when he began to drool. Blobby wasn't saving his adventurous spirit for the outdoors alone, and he decided to try some of their famous fluffy honey nut cream cheese on his bagel.

"This tastes more like dessert than breakfast!" he said.

Looking through a large window, they marveled at the busy bakers deftly rolling out homemade bagel dough. Blobby and his friends giggled at the sign overhead, wondering what might happen if one did feed the bakers. Their bagels were gone before Blobby could be tempted to entice the bakers with their own creations.

Image Optical
907-452-2024

Their next stop was Image Optical, so they could pick up Billy's new glasses. Blobby and his friends tried on all the different shapes, sizes, and colors of glasses the store offered.

"If I needed glasses, I would pick these!" Blobbette said, posing with a bright pink pair.

Blobby wasn't sure which he would have chosen, but he thought Blobbette's choice was a perfect fit for her. The cheery blobs working there were helpful, graciously answering all the blobs' various questions.

"Can we go see the Chena River?" Blobby asked as they left Image Optical. "I wonder if the trading post from the Gold Rush is still there!"

They loaded into their vehicles and made their way to First Avenue. Downtown Fairbanks lined the river, with buildings both new and old. Blobby didn't see the trading post, but he skipped happily along the path that followed the winding Chena River. Blobbette trailed behind with Billy, admiring the ducks as they gracefully paddled through the gently flowing water. Birch trees lined the path, and fireweed dotted the long grasses that grew down the steep riverbank. Blobby wished he could go gold panning in the river.

Maybe the Golden Heart is long forgotten, buried deep in the Chena River, he thought.

A few moments later, Blobby's thoughts of gold were interrupted when he spotted a fleet of rafts and canoes. He and Blobbette giggled with delight as the gaggle of happy blobs floated by.

Blobby overheard bits and pieces of the conversation between the moms about their next stop. He wasn't entirely sure where they were going, but it sounded like it would be a grand adventure. He knew for sure he heard the word "Quest."

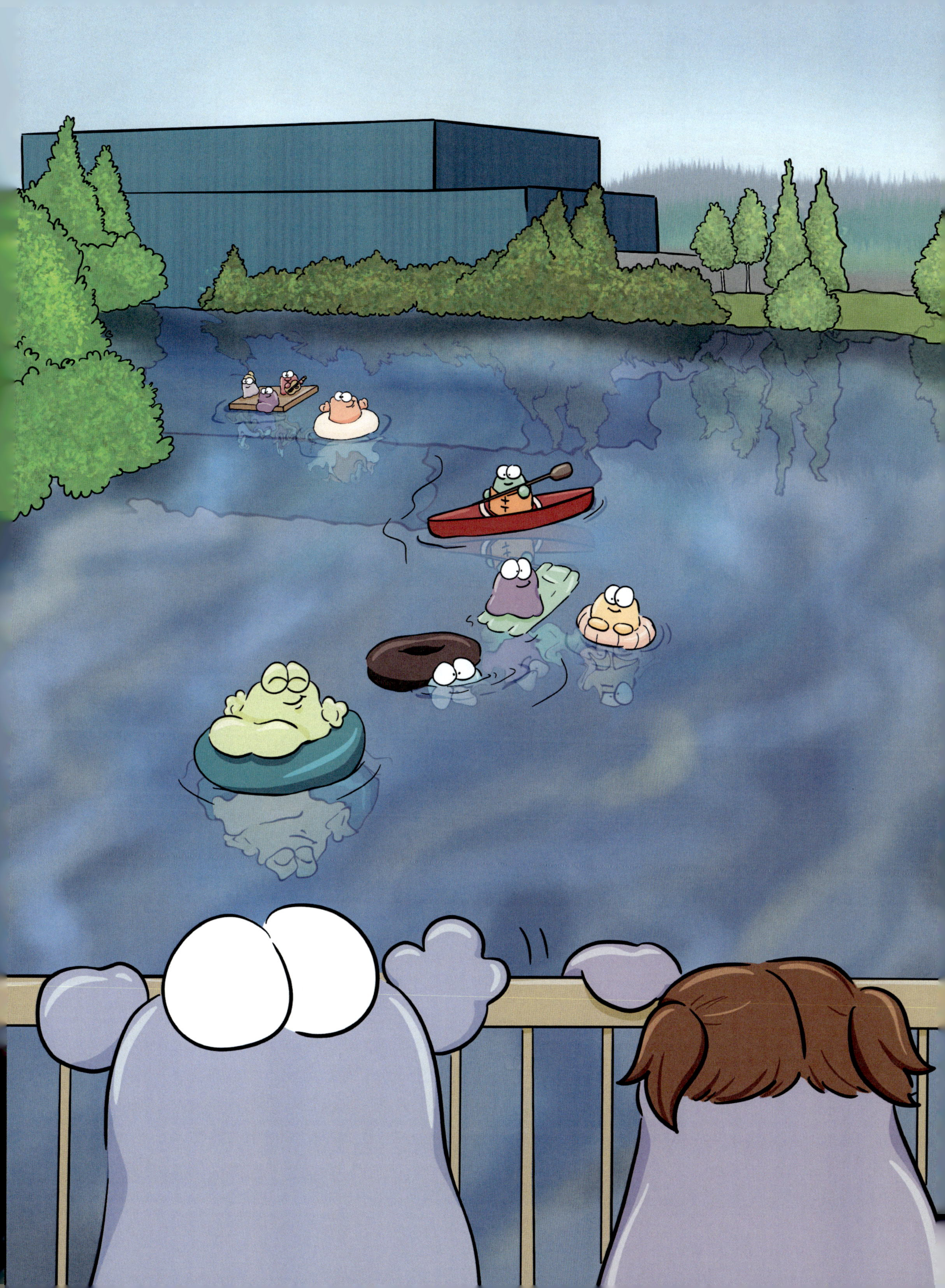

As they drove up to a bright yellow building, Blobby felt he might nearly burst with anticipation. The Toy Quest held all manner of treasures that a young blob would need to create, explore, and push their imaginations. The back corner held tables covered with toys for blobs to play with. Billy headed straight for the train set, while Blobby and Blobbette reveled at the walls covered with any toy they could want. Billy picked out a new train, Blobbette opted for the board game Hungry Hungry Blobs, and Blobby chose a small figure of a bear.

Billy got to pick lunch. As always, he decided on PIZZA! College Town Pizzeria was just down the road.

"Welcome, friends!" said a warm voice from the kitchen as they walked through the front doors. The aroma of freshly baked pizza wafted through the air, drawing the group to the front counter to order. Before they knew it, they were devouring a pepperoni pizza. When Blobby's mom took her first bite, the cheese stretched across the table, making the kids giggle. When he smelled the calzone Blobbette's mom ordered, Blobby decided he would try that next time.

The blobs were all fueled up and ready for a visit to Creamer's Field. It was a large refuge for migrating birds, with various trails meandering through the many acres of land dedicated to preservation and research.

Blobby peeked over the aged wooden fence that separated him from the tall grasses. Geese, cranes, and swans squawked and splashed in the pools of water that scattered the field. Blobby spied a bird nesting in the grasses a short distance away, and he was happy the birds had this sanctuary to depend on as the city grew around it.

Blobby and his friends picked up some abandoned sticks and headed off to explore the trails ahead. Blobby reminded his friends to keep an eye out for the Golden Heart.

"Don't go too far!" the moms called in tandem.

Sipping Streams
tea company

After hours of walking, exploring, and chatting, they began their walk back to the parking lot. Brooke gave Brenda a mischievous grin. "You know, if the kids liked the Chena River, they might enjoy Sipping Streams."

Blobby was puzzled. He knew it wasn't wise to sip the water from rivers and streams, but he trusted his friend's mom.

Blobby let out a sigh of relief when Brooke led him to a teahouse, where they sat down for a formal tea party. Blobby felt a warmth in his heart as Blobbette's face lit up. They were served a pot of tea, fresh fruit, salad, a variety of scones, pastries, and a tower of sandwiches.

"I feel so fancy!" Blobbette said as she sipped her tea.

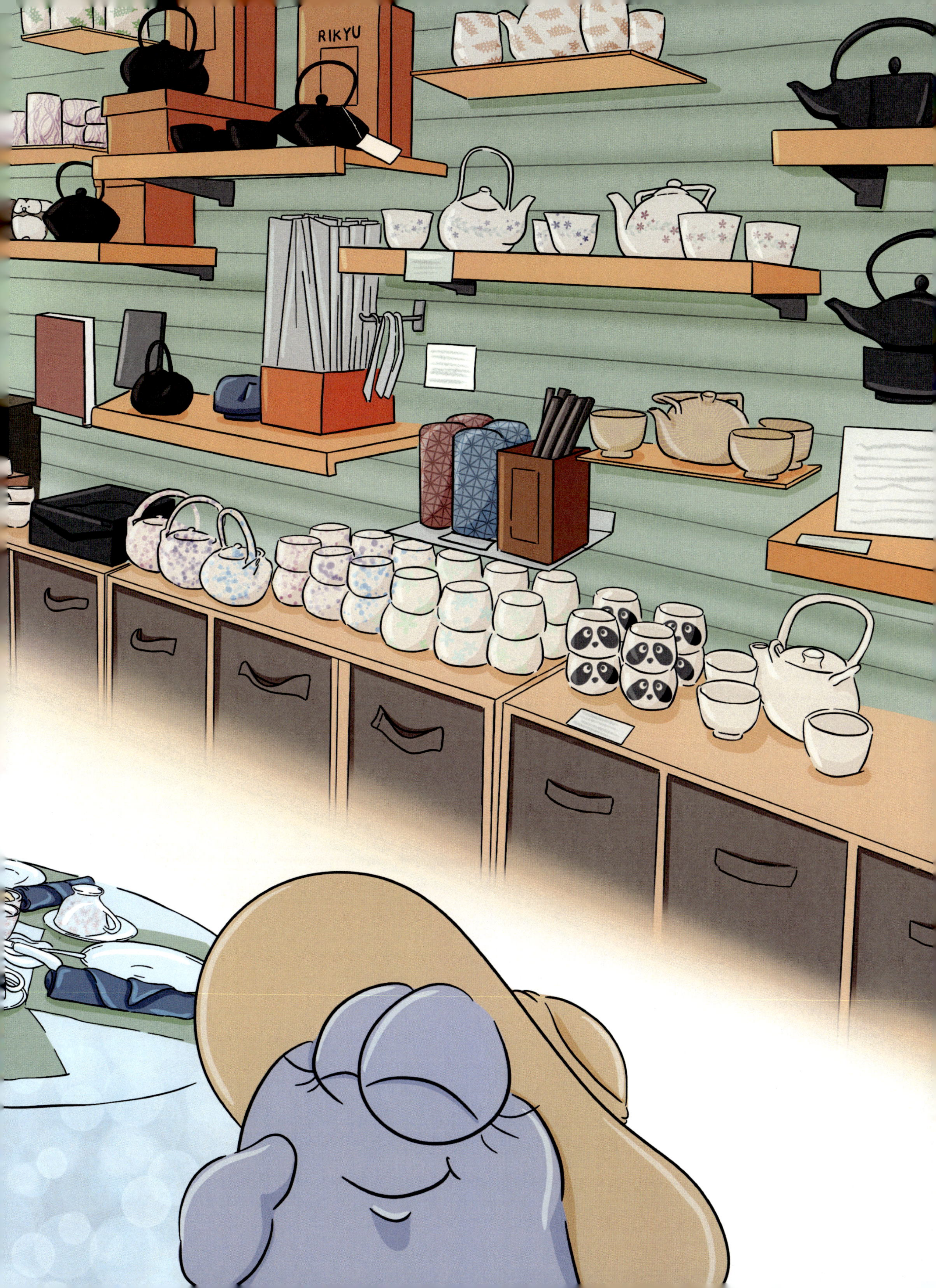
RIKYU

Near the end of their tea party, Billy nearly fell asleep, so the two families parted ways for the day.

"I'm not tired at all!" Blobby declared when his mom asked how he felt.

She nodded and took them to Georgeson Botanical Gardens. The gardens were filled with colorful flowers, trees, and lush grass. They happened to be there right on time for Music in the Park. Each week during the summer, talented blobs played music alongside the bees that buzzed through the foliage.

Nearing the end of the day, Blobby began to feel slightly disappointed. When his mom pressed him, he finally told her what weighed heavily on his mind.

"I thought I would be able to find the Golden Heart! I haven't seen even a speck of gold here."

Brenda paused thoughtfully and gave Blobby a gentle squeeze.

The following morning, Blobby woke with a plan in mind. He asked his mom for some paper and markers, then he proceeded to spend the morning creating a colorful flier. When he finally showed his mom, she beamed with pride at his grand idea.

After a stop at a drive-through coffee hut, they drove to 30th Avenue and arrived at Advance Printing. They were welcomed by Sir Pepper, the dog. "He's our official paper shredder, don't mind him!" called a blob from behind the counter. Blobby timidly approached the counter and held up his picture.

"Can you print more of these for me?" asked Blobby. "I'm trying to find the Golden Heart of Fairbanks!"

Not too long after, Blobby carried his stack of expertly printed flyers out to the car. He wondered where they might put them. Someone must know about the Golden Heart!

Their flier-posting mission led them all throughout Fairbanks, where they popped into Alaska Feed Company. Blobby was surprised that the large store had not only everything you'd need for your pets or livestock, but also a huge collection of Alaskan-made products.

"Let's pick out some things to bring back to our friends in Blobbington," said his mom.

Blobby picked out some jerky sticks, chocolates, barbeque sauce, and birch syrup. He shook his head when he saw his mom loaded up with fragrant soaps, lotions, tasty mints, jam, and more fresh coffee beans.

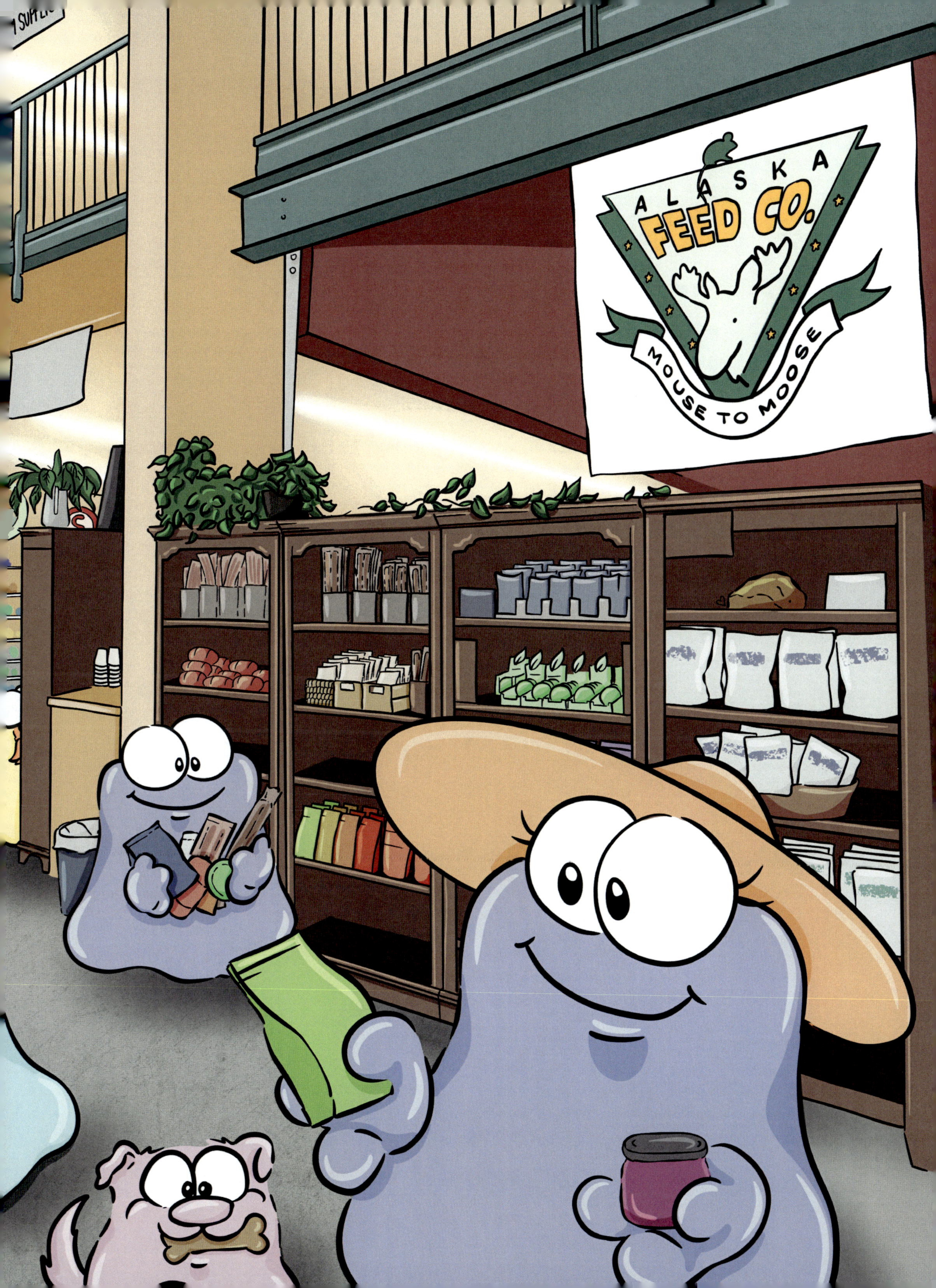
ALASKA
FEED CO.
MOUSE TO MOOSE

Blobby giggled under the pile of bags in the back seat as they drove to the Tanana Valley Farmers Market.

"I'd like to get some fresh vegetables for our next meal," Brenda said as they neared their next stop. "You can pick out some goodies, too!"

Northern Freeze Freeze Dried Candy and Fruits

The two blobs soon joined the crowds of cheery blobs exploring the market. Blobby was immediately drawn to a tent where freeze-dried candy and fruits were sold. He never realized such a thing could be done! There were freeze-dried chocolates, raspberries, and candy. The shopkeepers let him sample freeze-dried Skittles. They were light, crunchy, and fruity. Blobby found the first treat he wanted to get. He had never had a candy disintegrate in his mouth like this.

Blobby passed many tents, all filled with homemade items crafted and grown by various talented blobs. He marveled at the pottery, before his mom pulled him along to pick out some fresh tomatoes.

After they shuffled to the car, Blobby let out a big yawn. Brenda looked at him sideways.

"Tired already?" she asked.

Blobby nodded. "Shopping always wears me out."

"We can't have that," she said as they drove out of the parking lot. "We have a big day at the lake planned!"

That certainly perked Blobby up. "What lake? Where?" he asked as they drove.

"We're camping overnight at Chena Lakes," she said. "Brooke asked me to bring the meat for this afternoon. She and Robert are going to take care of everything else. They even got a new tent for tonight!"

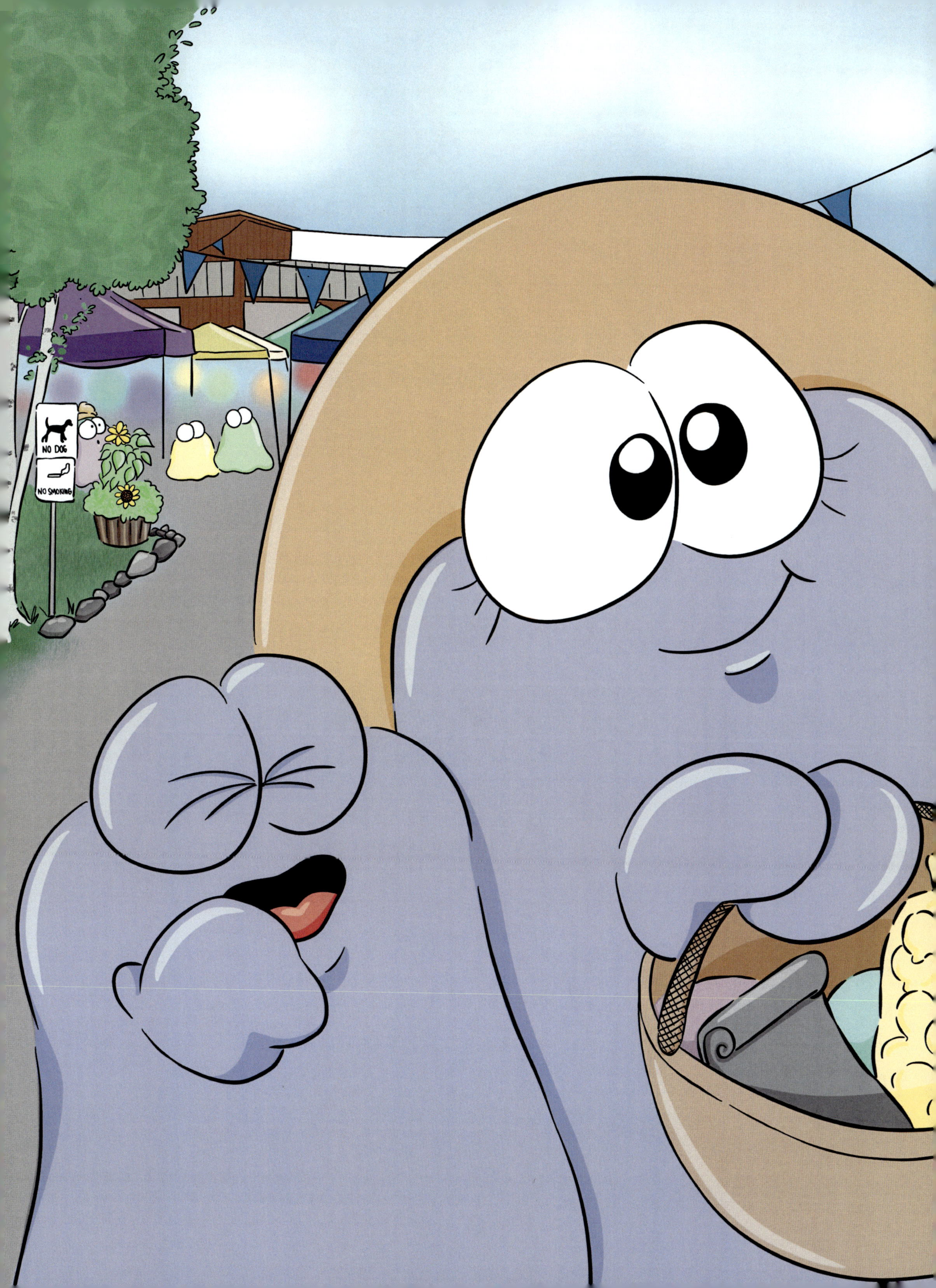
NO DOG
NO SMOKING

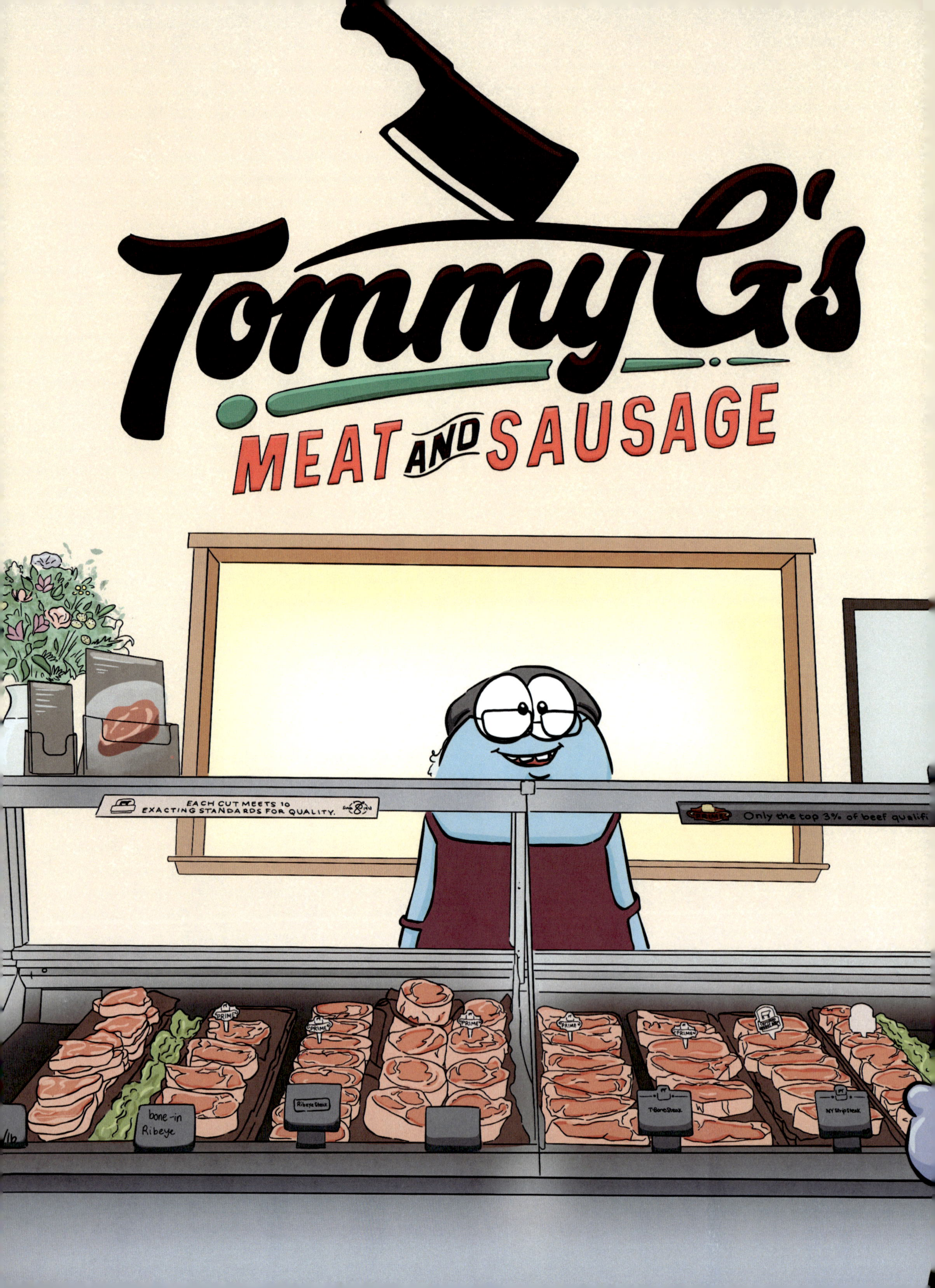

Tommy G's
MEAT AND SAUSAGE
EACH CUT MEETS 10 EXACTING STANDARDS FOR QUALITY.
PRIME
Only the top 3% of beef qualifi
PRIME
PRIME
PRIME
PRIME
PRIME
bone-in Ribeye
Ribeye Steak
T-Bone Steak
NY Strip Steak

Tommy G's Meat & Sausage was a sight to behold. Blobby pointed to the plump steaks in the glass case before him. "I think Mr. Robert would like that steak!"

Blobbette and Billy's dad was a kind, silly blob, with a fine taste for all foods. Blobby preferred a juicy hamburger, but he knew from the past that Robert liked a nice, marbled steak. On more than one family cookout, he had heard Robert discuss at length how important the proper cut of meat was. Blobby was happy when his mom pointed to the ribeye. She chose cheddar bratwurst for her and Brooke and Angus beef burgers for him and Blobbette.

They were finally at Chena Lakes! Robert immediately got the grill heated up and pulled out a small canister with a bright red lid.

"This here, Blobby," he whispered, "is my secret weapon. I never leave for a barbeque without Trueheart's Blend for beef. It's a delicious and healthy blend I feel good putting on my food. It has no MSG, gluten, fillers, or sugar—just all natural spices." Blobby didn't know what MSG, gluten, or fillers were, but if Mr. Robert didn't want them, then he didn't either.

Blobby was thankful Alaskan summer days were so long. He could fit more fun into every drop of sunlight. They kids waded into the water, splashing each other, while the adults grilled the meat over pleasant conversation. After they ate, Robert lay back to take a nap.

"Mr. Robert must have enjoyed his steak!" said Blobby.

"I'd say so," said Brooke as she patted her husband's full belly. "Once he wakes up, I'm sure he'll have some energy to take you three young ones on a jaunt around the lake."

While Robert napped, Blobby, Billy, and Blobbette tossed pebbles into the glimmering water. Billy skipped a smooth stone four times before it sank into the water, initiating an impromptu rock skipping competition. The screams and shouts of glee cut Robert's nap short, and he plodded his way to the kids.

"Alright, kids," he said, rubbing his hands together. "Are you ready for an adventure?"

The kids, already amped up from throwing rocks, screamed in unison.

The moms shook their heads, laughing. "We'll set the tent up while you're out. Have fun!"

Blobby followed Robert as he journeyed to the paths winding around the lake. The other kids trailed behind him like little ducklings. They hunted for snails and made them small homes with wet sand and sticks.

"My snails will love their new home!" Blobby said proudly. Blobbette nodded in agreement.

Blobby hadn't noticed the canoe tied up nearby until Robert pulled out three small lifejackets. They loaded into the canoe as Robert snapped on his larger lifejacket. Blobby sat very still as Robert paddled out to the center of the lake. He learned quickly that too much wiggling made the canoe wobbly. He and his friends were silent as they glided across the lake. He imagined he was a fish, skimming the water's surface.

Once the canoe ride was over, Blobby spent the remainder of the day playing with his friends in the lake. When they tired of swimming, they dried out on the playground near the water. The moms called them back to the campsite, where they had prepared a small campfire. Blobby sniffed the air. "Do I smell marshmallows?"

Blobby spent the rest of the evening expertly roasting raw marshmallows to golden perfection as Robert told campfire stories. Each time Billy tried to toast his marshmallow, it turned to a ball of fire before falling into the flames. Blobbette and Billy happily let Blobby roast the marshmallows.

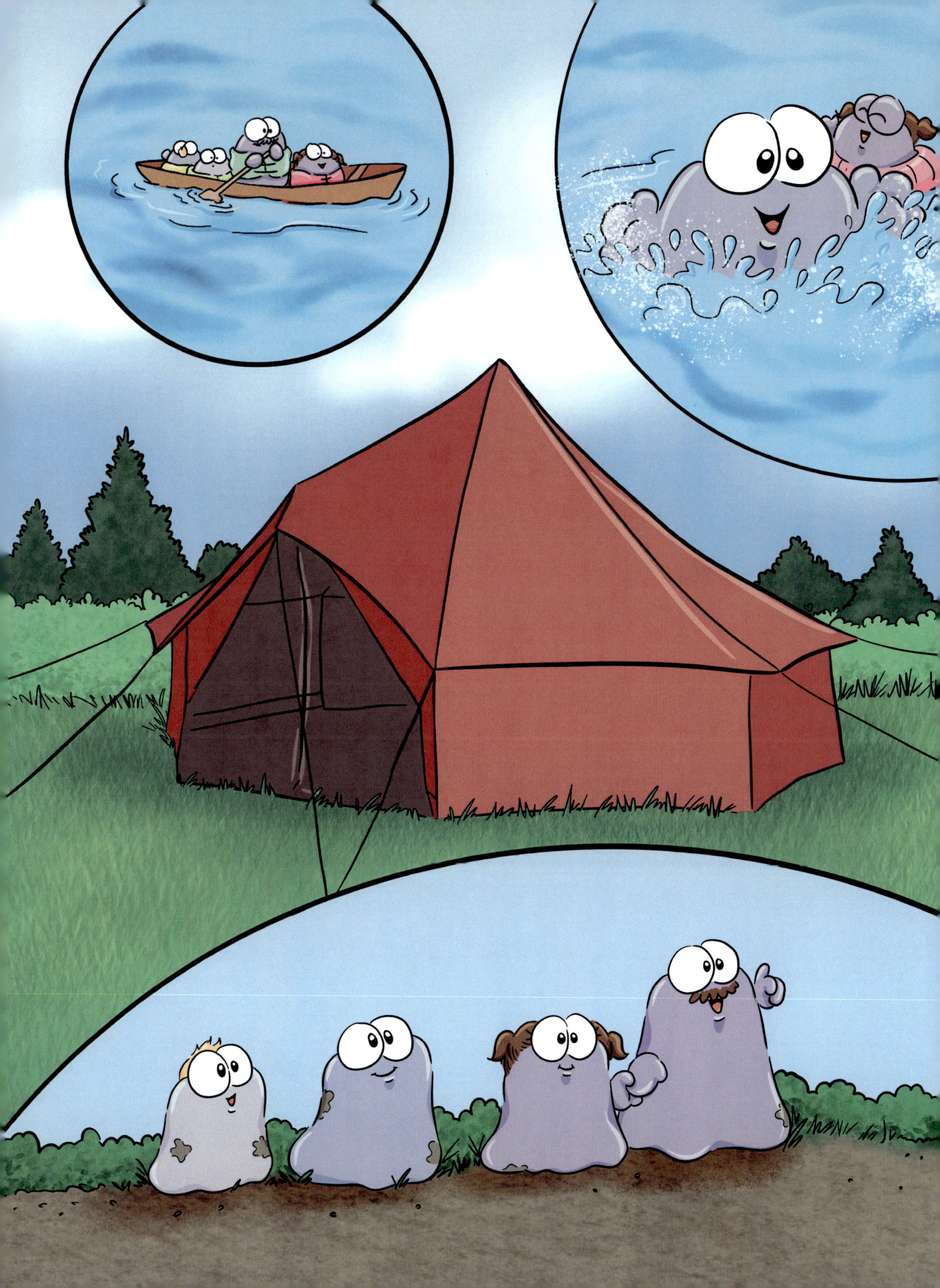

The next morning, Blobby and his mom drove back to their rental. He gladly showered off, and when he went to the living room, he found his mom had packed some water bottles, a small first aid kit, a towel, and some snacks in his backpack.

"We're headed to Angel Rocks this afternoon, so I put together our day pack!" she announced.

Before the 48-mile trip on Chena Hot Springs Road, they stopped at Larae's for some freshly made cinnamon rolls, chewy chocolate chip cookies, and lemon scones.

As the bright sunshine came in through Larae's windows, it cast a warm glow over the blobs. Blobby looked at those around him, glad he was here with his favorite blobs. *How good it is to be with friends,* he thought as he stirred his chocolate milk. He took a sip and let out a happy sigh. Delicious.

The hike up Angel Rocks was a new experience for all the blobs. It started easily, a gentle path curving along the hill as it slowly climbed higher. The wind picked up, and the sun hid behind the clouds, giving them a fresh sense of adventure. The breeze kept the mosquitoes away, and the coolness helped them as they reached the steep incline to the top of the rock formations. Blobby was worn out by the time they reached the top, and he wasn't the only one. Robert carried Blobby on his back for the final stretch.

After a snack break, they found the energy to climb further and explore the cave at the top. The view was utterly breathtaking! The sun finally broke out from behind the clouds, lighting up the granite rock formations. The Chena River flowed far below them, snaking through the landscape. An army of spruce trees dotted the hillsides, interspersed with clusters of birch trees. Blobby could see a burned patch across the valley from where a forest fire had recently scorched the land.

The journey back down to the cars seemed much faster than the journey to the top. Billy snoozed on Robert's back as he lumbered down the well-worn path. Blobby counted how many squirrels he saw, while Blobbette kept a keen eye out for moose.

By the time they got back to Fairbanks, it was late afternoon. Blobby and Brenda parted ways from their friends for a night of rest.

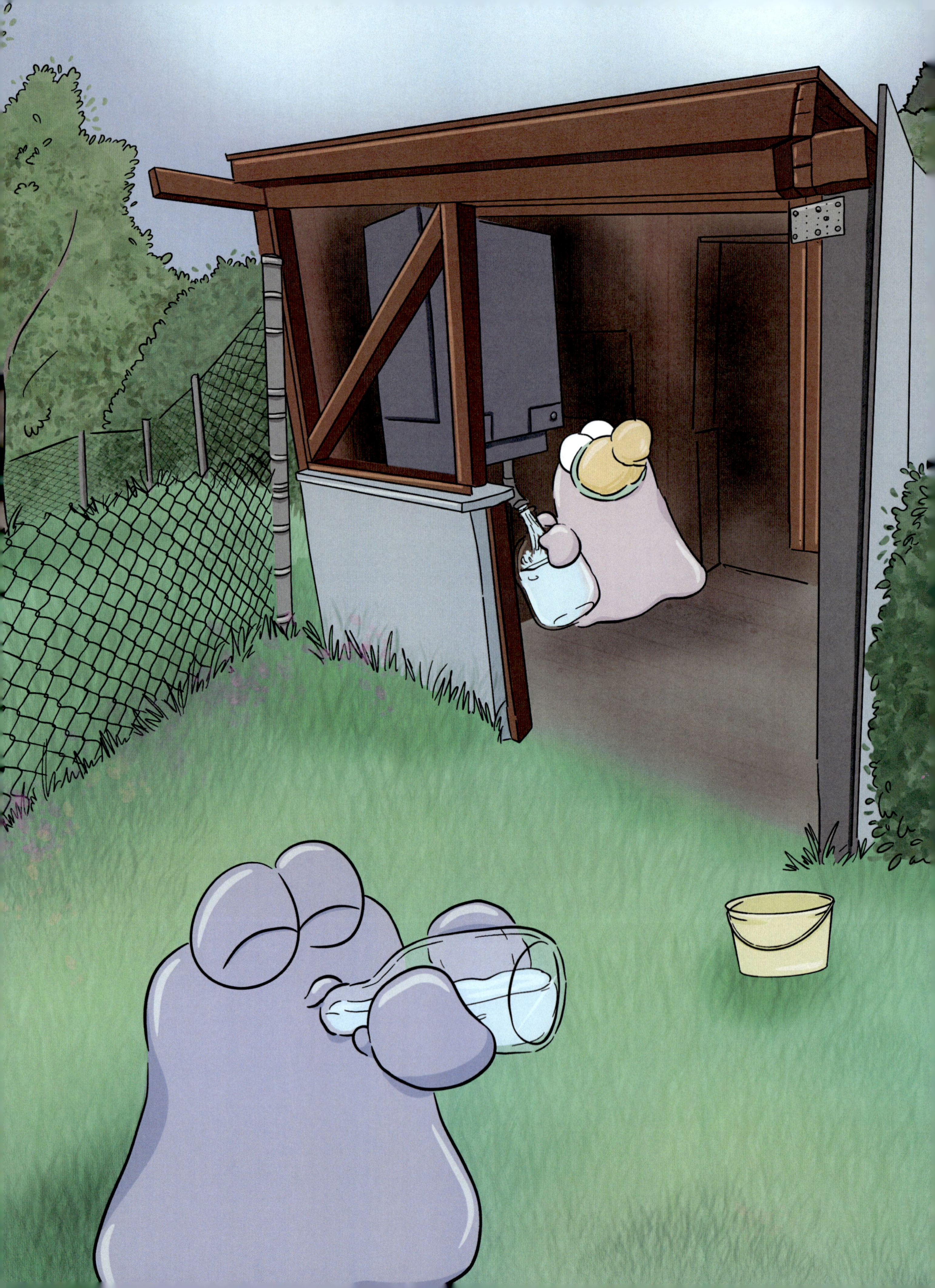

The next day everyone met near Fox, a small town northwest of Fairbanks.

"I know this is strange," Brooke laughed as she led the kids to a little worn building near the roadside. "This is the Fox Spring. It may not look like much, but this is the best place to get the most amazing tasting water."

It seemed an odd thing to be known for, but Blobby filled his water bottle and took a sip. It was only water, but Blobby had never tasted water so refreshing and crisp in his entire life.

Looking around, Blobby was puzzled that his friends had brought empty buckets as well as water bottles. He realized why when they led him to a large raspberry patch.

"You can find these patches all over if you know where to look!" Brooke said as she handed the kids each a bucket.

They spent the morning filling their buckets, but somehow the little blob's buckets never seemed to get very full.

As they walked back to their car, Blobby heard his mom's phone *ding*. "Blobby, we've got a message about the gold!" she exclaimed.

"What does it say?!" Blobby asked as he attempted to peek over her shoulder, trying to read the message.

If your heart seeks gold by hand to weigh, go to 1671 Steese Highway.

But if real treasure is your ambition, 725 26th Avenue should be your mission.

"Well! Isn't that interesting." Brenda said slowly. "Should we see where this leads us?"

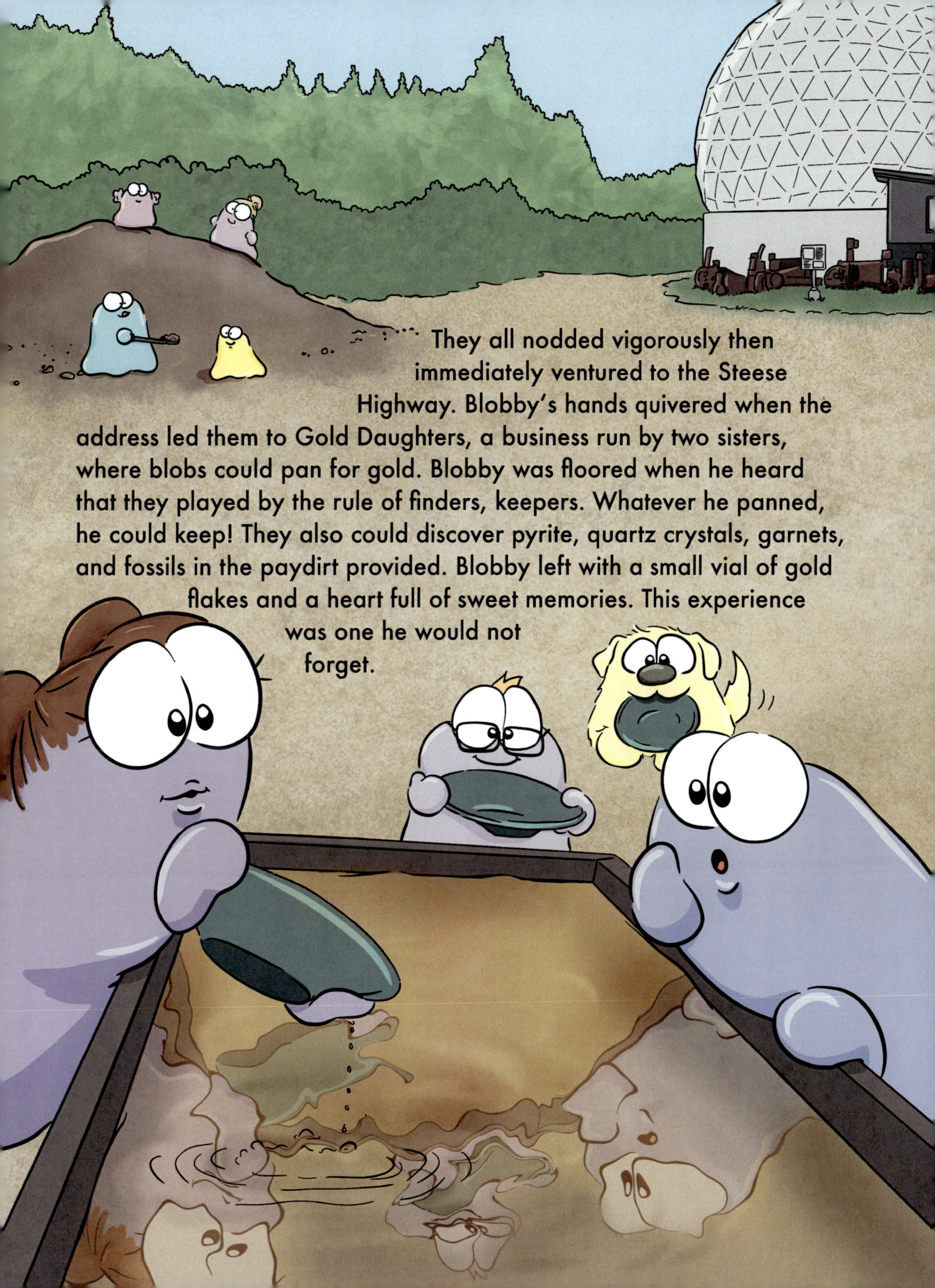

They all nodded vigorously then immediately ventured to the Steese Highway. Blobby's hands quivered when the address led them to Gold Daughters, a business run by two sisters, where blobs could pan for gold. Blobby was floored when he heard that they played by the rule of finders, keepers. Whatever he panned, he could keep! They also could discover pyrite, quartz crystals, garnets, and fossils in the paydirt provided. Blobby left with a small vial of gold flakes and a heart full of sweet memories. This experience was one he would not forget.

As they drove back to their rental, they made one last stop to see the Alaska Pipeline. It transported oil the eight hundred miles from up north to the small town of Valdez.

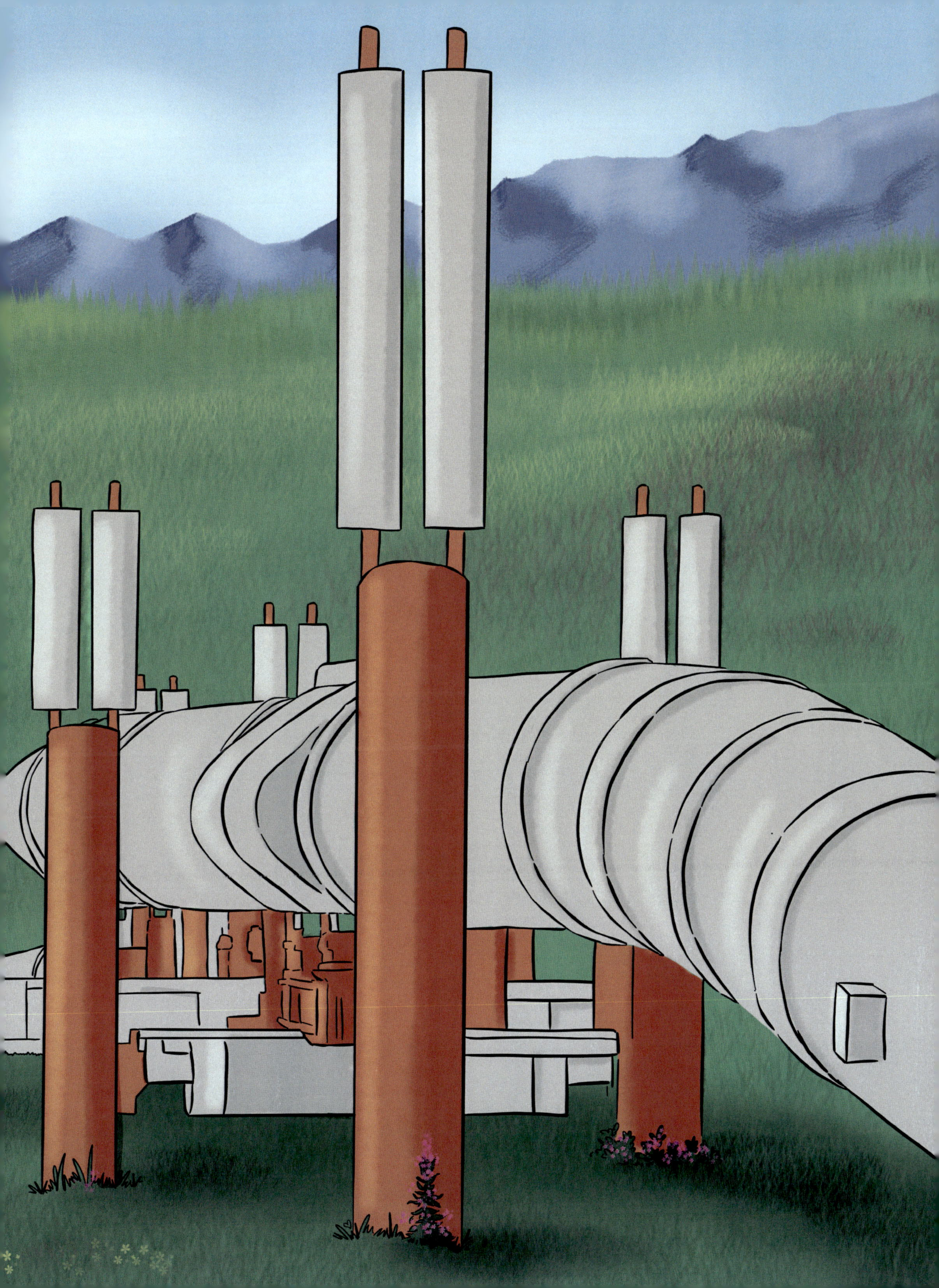

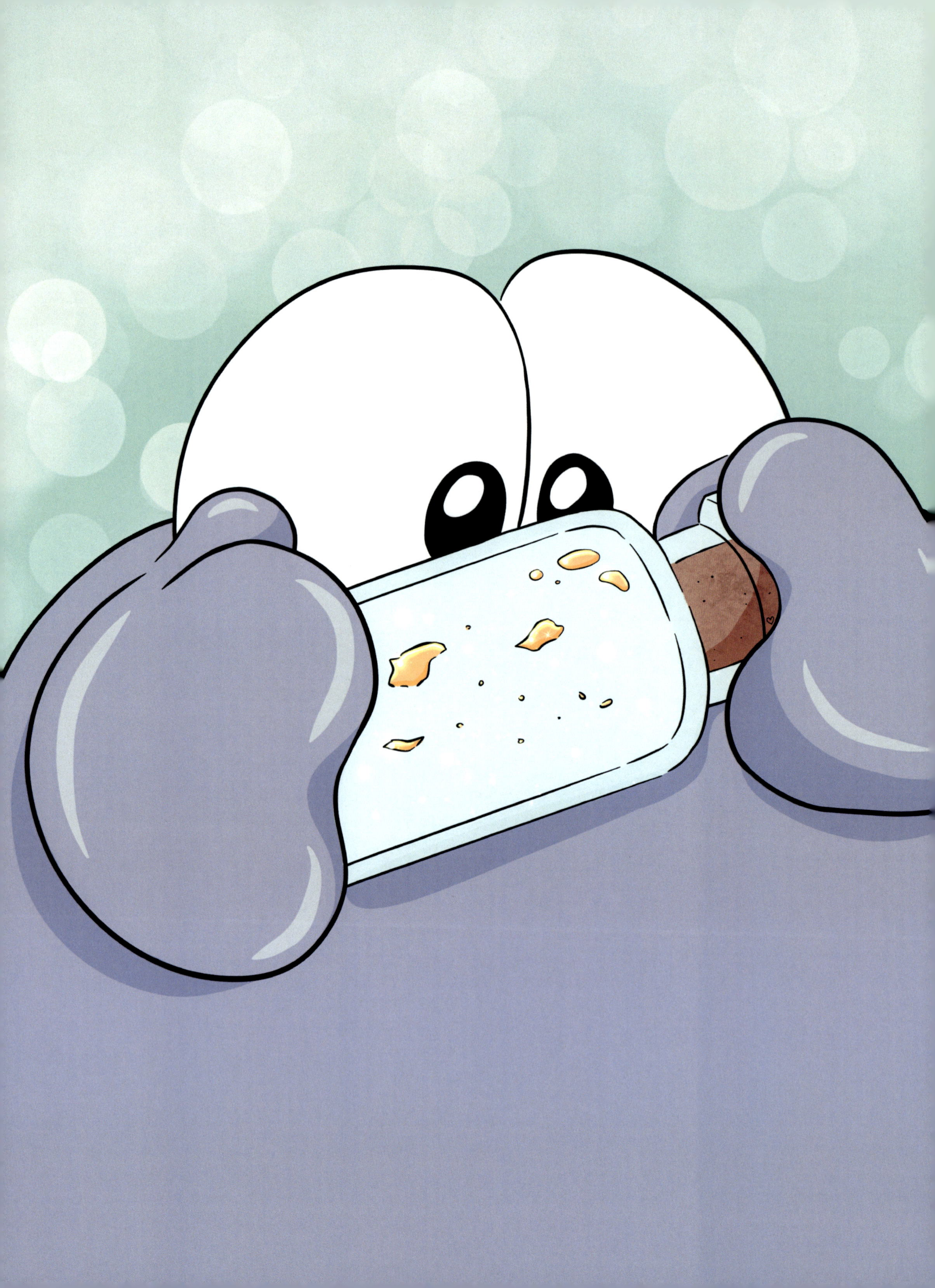

As Blobby lay in bed, he gazed at the bottled gold flakes in his hand. As he flipped the small bottle over, the gold sparkled as it sank to the bottom. He couldn't help but wonder what the mystery Blob's text message about "real treasure" meant. Hadn't he already found real treasure?

He didn't have to wonder long, because the next time he opened his eyes, it was morning. His mom was just as curious as he was, and 725 26th Avenue was their first destination. Blobby studied the building that the message said held great treasure. He was puzzled. It didn't look like a place you would find gold. They went inside to investigate.

As they entered, the blobs they encountered greeted them. "Hello! Welcome to the Fairbanks Community Food Bank!"

Blobby was amazed by how the community came together to help hungry blobs who did not always have enough to eat. "We collect and redistribute donated food to individuals and agencies throughout the city," said one of the volunteers. "We want to help feed hungry blobs. Anyone can help us!"

As they drove away from the Food Bank, Blobby and his mom were silent. Blobby saw tears welling up in his mom's eyes, and she squeezed his hand. He hadn't thought about what it might feel like to go without a meal. It made him sad, but it also fueled his desire to help others.

On their way home, Blobby saw a Meals on Wheels truck stop at a house and a kind blob dropping a big red bag off at a little old blob's home. The bag said "LUNCH." Blobby was beginning to see that the treasures of Fairbanks were not something shiny to find in a pan but in the hearts of those who were willing to help others.

They had seen that kindness at every place they had visited. Blobby and Brenda went to their rental that evening with the warmth of realization glowing in their hearts.

The next day brought an Alaskan thunderstorm. The thunder clapped overhead, and the sun refracted through the raindrops as they dropped heavily to the ground.
Blobby gaped at the sky. "This is magical!"

Though the rain was peaceful, Blobby and his mom decided to visit the Morris Thompson Cultural and Visitors Center, where they got to tour life-sized dioramas depicting the seasons. Through the exhibits, they visited a rural fish camp, saw a grizzly bear digging for ground squirrels, and peered through a cabin window in the winter.

"ROOOAR! I'm a bear! Give me a squirrel!" Blobby growled as they left.

Next, they tried virtual reality at Arctic Sun VR. Once he had watched a quick video with instructions on how to play, Blobby chose to play as a chef, flipping hamburgers. Next, he fought in epic battles as an archer and then finished off floating in a bright whimsical world as he tried to eat little shapes. Each shape he ate made his virtual tail grow longer and longer.

He'd always loved video games, but this was an immersive experience he knew he wanted to return to.

The remainder of their trip was filled with time spent with their friends. They walked the numerous paths for the Trails Challenges, making sure to stop at each sign and take a picture to commemorate that they'd been there. They ate at fun restaurants and enjoyed the places they'd already visited once before but needed to experience again.

As their departure drew closer, the weight on their hearts grew heavier. "I feel like I'm going to leave part of myself behind," Blobby sighed. His mom nodded.

FAIRBANKS
TRAILS
CHALLENGE
EAGLE TRAIL
#1
#FNSBtrails
TANANA LAKES RECREATION AREA

Before flying back to Blobbington, Blobby found himself tagging along with his mom as she met with a realtor. "Blobby, this is Michelle Evans. She's going to show us a few homes in the area."

They visited numerous houses, all of which Blobby couldn't feel comfortable in. That was, until the last house. It was a red house with a large yard and lots of big bushy trees. Blobby imagined running through the forest, rolling in the grass, and what the room he'd picked for himself would look like. It had some things that needed to be fixed, but Blobby was willing to help.

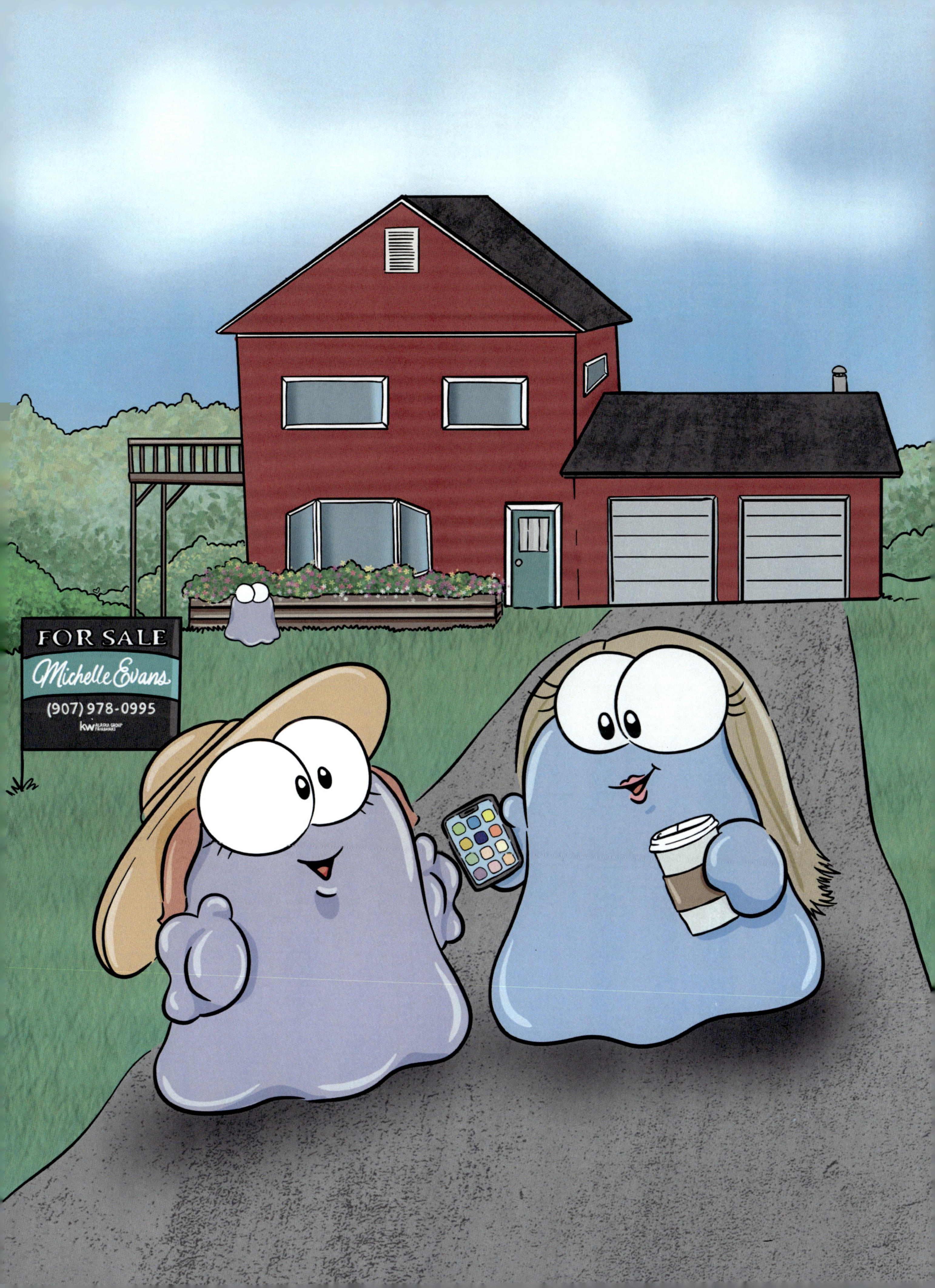
FOR SALE
Michelle Evans
(907) 978-0995

In the following days, Brenda carted Blobby around town. They spent quite some time at Mt. McKinley Bank, where his mom was tasked with signing a mountain of papers. He wanted to draw on some of the paper, but the loan officer behind the desk told him those papers were very important. Blobby was glad he brought Bubby to keep him company.

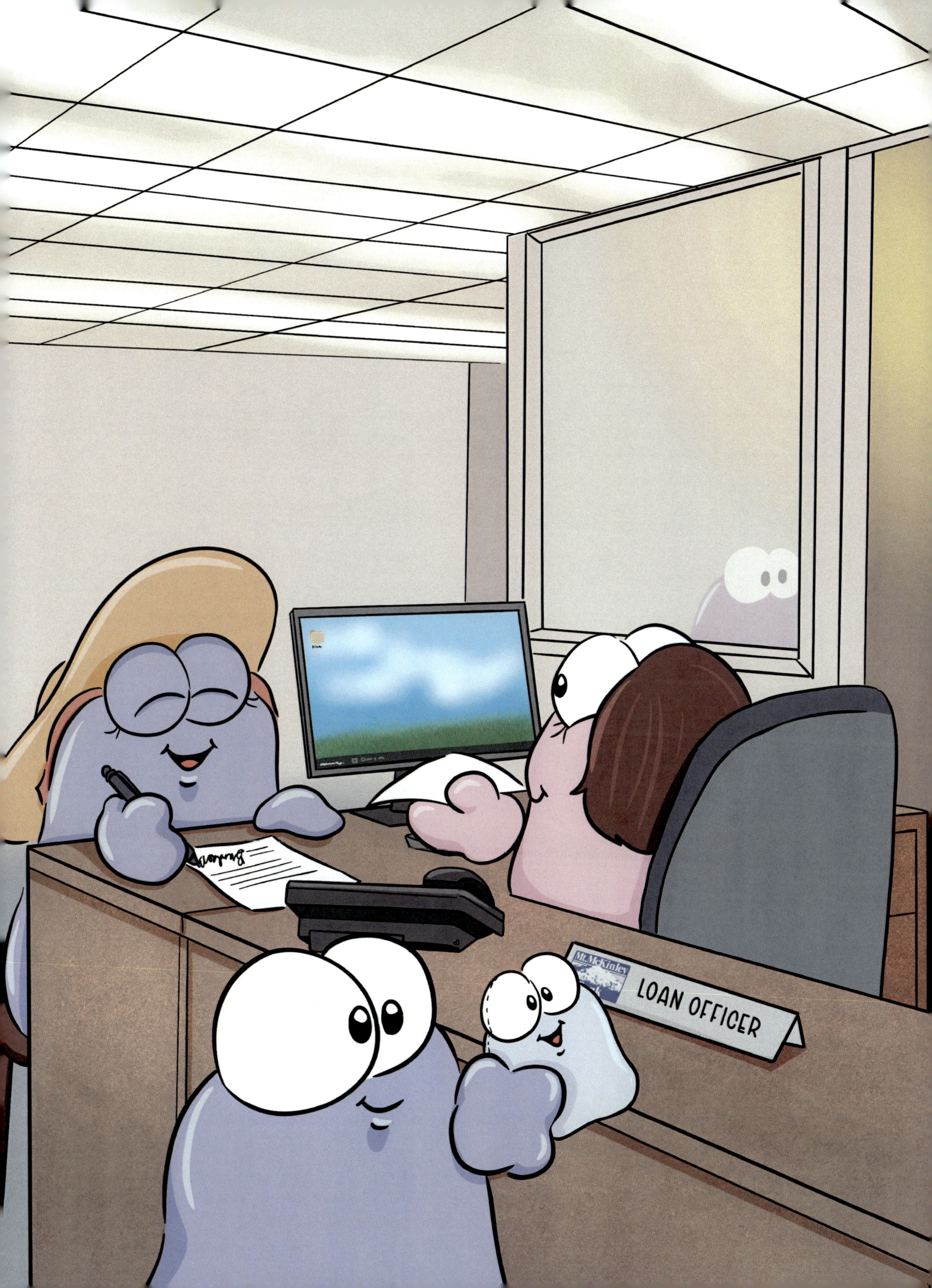
Mt. McKinley
LOAN OFFICER

Time passed, and they soon returned to Blobbington. "It feels strange," Blobby said as they stepped into their old apartment. "This doesn't feel like home anymore."

Brenda nodded with a small smile. "It won't be for much longer." She set out some boxes, and they began the process of moving their life to Alaska.

After many long days driving, a flat tire, snack breaks, tears, and laughter, Blobby and his mom arrived safely in Fairbanks. This time, their adventure led them through Canada, where they saw many bears and moose along the road.

Their house was ready for them to move in, but Brenda stopped by Independent Rental to rent a few things to prepare the house. Blobby was disappointed that his mom didn't rent the mini excavator. He imagined digging for gold with it in his new backyard. He understood the more pressing need to use the carpet shampooer, though.

INDEPENDENT
IR
RENTAL
"We're here to Help"
456-6595
IR
RENTAL RETURNS
RENTAL RETURNS
EQUIPMENT RENTAL
PARTY SUPPLIES
TENTS, TABLES AND CHAIRS
INDOOR/OUTDOOR STORAGE
SMALL ENGINE REPAIR

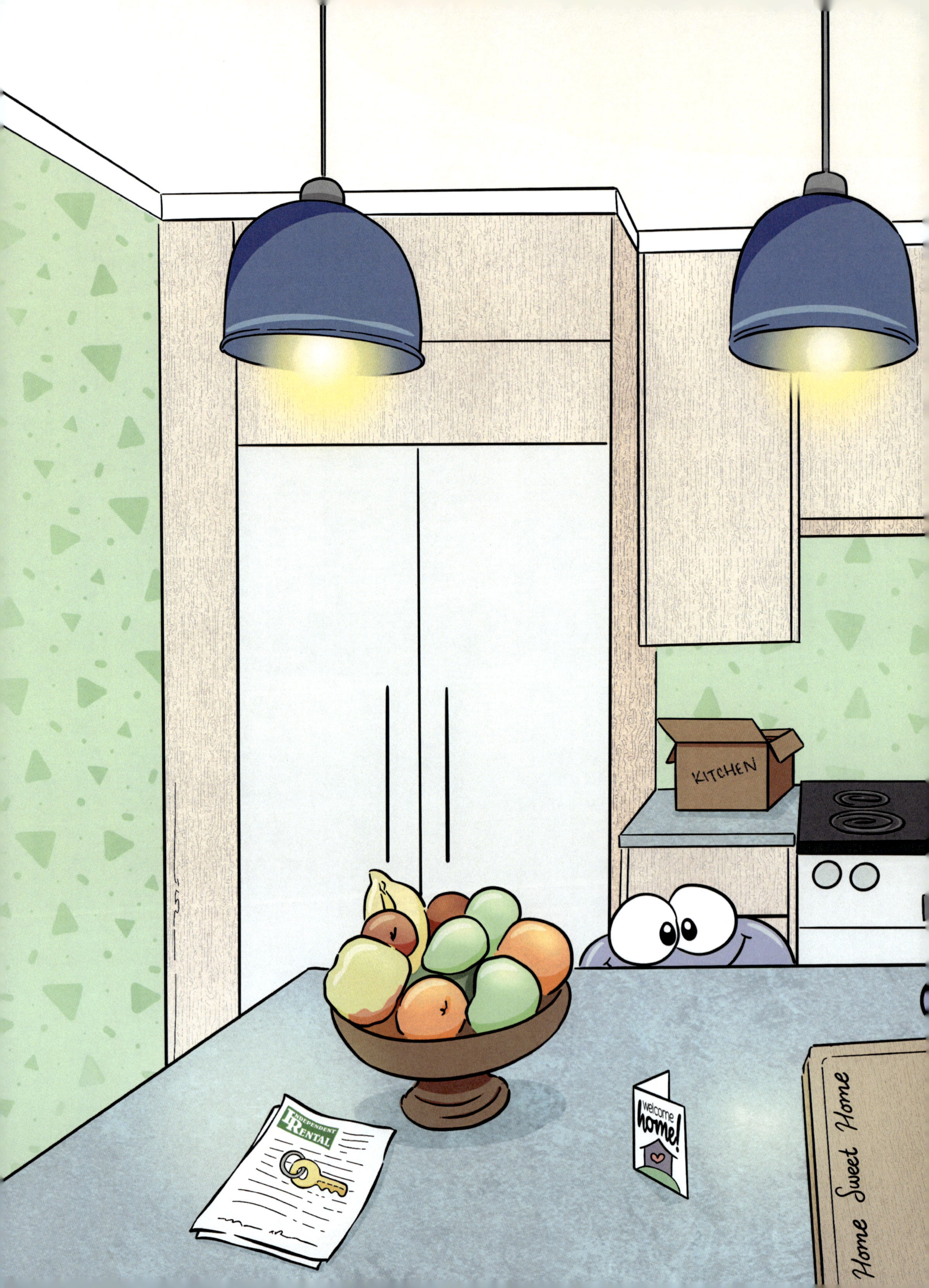
KITCHEN
INDEPENDENT
RENTAL
welcome
home!
Home Sweet Home

After moving in, Michelle gifted them with a cutting board engraved by Fairbanks Award Makers. That gave Blobby an idea! They had been searching for a way to commemorate the experience that led them to move to Fairbanks. "Can we get something to engrave for our welcome home present to ourselves?" Blobby asked eagerly.

"That's a great idea, Sweetie," Brenda said, giving him a squeeze.

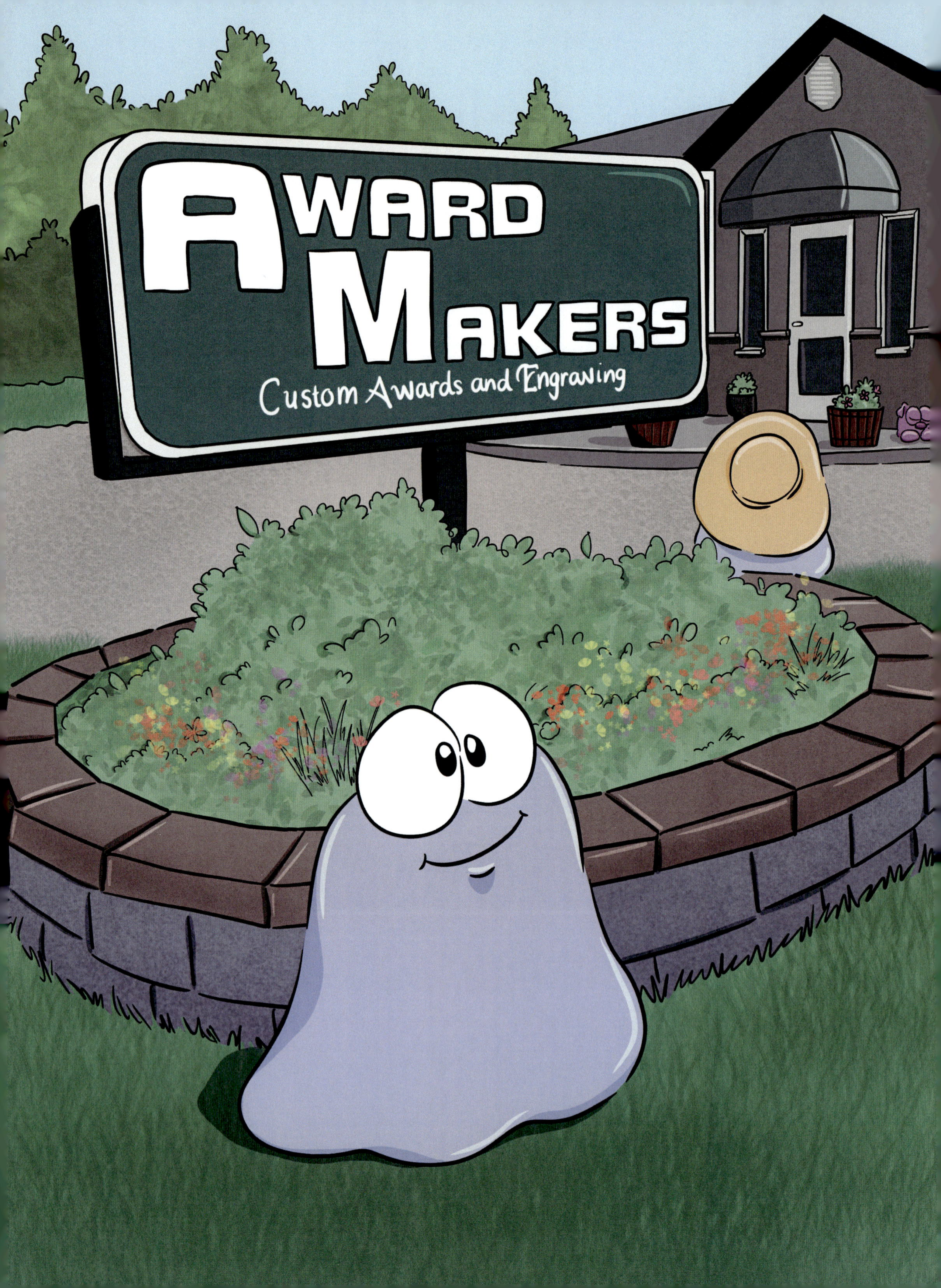
AWARD MAKERS
Custom Awards and Engraving

They drove to Fairbanks Award Makers, where Blobby picked out a gold pan. Blobby was amazed at the wood, leather, glass, metal, and jewelry they engraved. The blobs there happily agreed to engrave the special poem he had written on the long drive to Fairbanks.

A few days later, the blobs picked up their custom engraved gold pan. Throughout their trip, Blobby had sought the Golden Heart of Fairbanks. He had been searching for something shiny, weighty, and magnificent to behold.

Blobby held the gold pan to his chest and he looked up to his mom. "I did discover the Golden Heart of Fairbanks, and it was more precious than anything we could have dug from the ground. It was in the hearts of the blobs we met!"

He sighed contentedly, eager to begin the new adventure they just embarked on.

FROM THE EARTH WE FIND GOLD THAT IS PRECIOUS, TREASURED AND PURE.

BUT IN THE HEART WE SEE KINDNESS, HOPE, AND A LOVE THAT ENDURES.

The end

INDEX

ADVANCE PRINTING
612 30th Avenue
Fairbanks, Alaska 99701
(907) 451-1111
www.hotprinter.com

ALASKA AUTO RENTAL
2375 University Avenue
Fairbanks, Alaska 99709
(907) 457-7368
www.alaskaautorental.com

ALASKA FEED COMPANY
1600 College Road
Fairbanks, Alaska 99709
(907) 451-5570
www.alaskafeed.com

ALASKA.LIZZIE
Follow me on Instagram & TikTok
for fun things to do in the Fairbanks area!

ANGEL ROCKS TRAIL
48.9 Chena Hot Springs Road
https://dnr.alaska.gov/parks/
maps/angelrockstrail.pdf

ARCTIC SUN VR
1800 Airport Way
Fairbanks, Alaska 99701
(907) 456-2787 (ASVR)
www.arcticsunvr.com

AURORA ARCHWAY
Over the road as you exit
Fairbanks International Airport

AWARD MAKERS
815 Airport Way
Fairbanks, Alaska 99701
(907) 456-8661
www.fairbanksawardmakers.com

CHENA LAKES RECREATION AREA
3780 Laurance Road
North Pole, Alaska 99705
(907) 488-1655
https://fairbanksak.myrec.com

**CHENA RIVER
STATE RECREATION SITE**
3530 Geraghty Avenue
Fairbanks, Alaska
https://fairbanksak.myrec.com

COLLEGE TOWN PIZZERIA
3535 College Road, Suite 103
Fairbanks, Alaska 99709
(907) 457-2200
www.ctownpizza.com

CREAMER'S FIELD & DAIRY
Farmhouse Visitor Center
1300 College Rd
Fairbanks, Alaska 99709
(907) 459-7307
www.friendsofcreamersfield.org

EXPLORE FAIRBANKS
101 Dunkel Street, Suite 111
Fairbanks, AK 99701
(907) 456-5774
www.explorefairbanks.com

FAIRBANKS TRAILS CHALLENGE
https://fairbanksak.myrec.com

FAIRBANKS COMMUNITY FOOD BANK
725 26th Avenue
Fairbanks, Alaska 99701
(907) 457-4273
www.fairbanksfoodbank.org

FOX SPRING
2331 Elliott Highway
Fox, Alaska
https://dot.alaska.gov/nreg/foxspring

GEORGESON BOTANICAL GARDENS
2180 West Tanana Drive
Fairbanks, Alaska 99775
www.georgesonbotanicalgarden.org

GOLD DAUGHTERS
1671 Steese Highway
Fairbanks, Alaska 99712
(907) 347-4749
www.golddaughters.com

IMAGE OPTICAL
1867 Airport Way, Suite 100
Fairbanks, Alaska 99701
(907) 452-2024
www.imageopticalalaska.com

INDEPENDENT RENTAL
2020 South Cushman Street
Fairbanks, Alaska 99701
(907) 456-6595
www.independentrental.com

LARAES BREADS, PIES & ESPRESSO
(off Chena Hot Springs Road)
696 Dahl Lane
Fairbanks, Alaska 99712
(907) 488-0948
www.laraesbpe.com

LITTLE RICHARD'S FAMILY DINER
2698 Hurst Road
North Pole, Alaska 99705
(907) 488-2117
www.littlerichardsfamilydiner.com

LULU'S BREAD & BAGELS
364 Old Chena Pump Road
Fairbanks, Alaska 99709
(907) 374 3804
www.lulusbagels.com

MEALS ON WHEELS
FAIRBANKS SENIOR CENTER
1424 Moore Street
Fairbanks, Alaska 99701
(907) 452-1735
www.fairbanksseniorcenter.org

MICHELLE EVANS REALTOR
KELLER WILLIAMS ALASKA GROUP
1292 Sadler Way, Suite 200
Fairbanks, Alaska 99701
(907) 978-0995
www.fairbanksdeltahomes.com

**MORRIS THOMPSON
CULTURAL & VISITORS CENTER**
101 Dunkel Street
Fairbanks, Alaska 99701
(907) 459.3700
www.morristhompsoncenter.org

MT. McKINLEY BANK
5 Locations to Serve You
Main Office
500 Fourth Avenue
Fairbanks, Alaska 99701
www.mtmckinleybank.com

NORTH POLE LAKESIDE CABINS
2510 Singa Street
North Pole, Alaska 99705
(907) 750-0360
www.nplscabins.com

NORTHERN FREEZE
(907) 750-9920
NorthernFreezeAK.com

PIONEER PARK
2300 Airport Way
Fairbanks, Alaska 99701
(907) 459-1087
www.pioneerpark.us

PIPELINE VIEWING
TRANS ALASKA PIPELINE
8.4 Mile Steese Highway
www.alyeska-pipe.com

RASPBERRY PICKING
Pick your own at
ANNS GREENHOUSES
780 Sheep Creek Road
Fairbanks, Alaska 99709
(907) 479-6921

RIVER CITY CAFÉ
in Co-op Plaza
535 2nd Avenue
Fairbanks, Alaska 99701
(907) 456-6242
www.rivercitycafefairbanks.com

SANTA CLAUS HOUSE
101 St. Nicholas Dr.
North Pole, Alaska 99705
(907) 488-2200
www.santaclaushouse.com

SIPPING STREAMS TEA COMPANY
374 Old Chena Pump Road
Fairbanks, Alaska 99709
1 855 TEAS4US (832-7487)
www.sippingstreams.com

TANANA LAKES RECREATION AREA
4400 S Cushman Street Ext
Fairbanks, Alaska 99701
(907) 459-1070
https://fairbanksak.myrec.com

TANANA VALLEY FARMERS MARKET
Located at the corner of
2600 College Road in Fairbanks, Alaska
Phone: (907) 456-3276
www.tvfmarket.com

THE TOY QUEST
2801 College Road
Fairbanks, Alaska 99709
(907) 479-7335
thetoyquest.com

TOMMY G'S MEAT & SAUSAGE
3290 Peger Road, Suite C
Fairbanks, AK 99709
(907) 450-9500
www.tommygsalaska.com

TRUEHEART'S BLEND SPICES
(907) 750-4310
www.trueheartsblend.com

EXTRAS

Can you find the tiny hearts sprinkled throughout the book?

How many Lizzie Blobs can you find?

Alaska.Lizzie on Instagram!

ABOUT THE BLOB LADY

Juliana Miller is a professional blob artist who resides in North Pole, Alaska with her husband and their two children.

After discovering her love for art at the age of two, Juliana has been drawing ever since. She also loves to teach children the foundations for emotional and physical health. When she is not creating art, you will likely find her reading a book, playing the piano, or enjoying a board game with her family. She loves Jesus, a hot cup of coffee, and a good conversation.

Blobs originated one fateful day in middle school Biology while Juliana was looking under a microscope at a cheek cell. She was tasked with drawing what she saw, so she sketched the amoebic shape. She felt that it needed something extra so she did what every self-respecting eighth grader would do and added googly eyes.

That day in science class, the blob was born. It was pretty cute, so she continued doodling them in other classes as well. With small adjustments and accessories, blobs were easily customizable. Soon, she was drawing classmates and teachers as blobs.

As she grew older, she continued to doodle and paint blobs for fun. Friends and family were amused, but it wasn't until she was illustrating and publishing other people's books that she began to wonder how others might receive them.

After participating in a few local bazaars, she found that blobs were adored by adults and children alike. Juliana is constantly amazed that her childhood doodles turned into a joyful way to connect with others.

Hi friends!

I hope you enjoyed my adventure in the Golden Heart City. I met so many new blobs! If you get a chance to visit them, send me a postcard! I'd love to hear from you!

Blobby

To: Blobby
PO Box 55742
North Pole, AK
99705

KEEP READING WITH THE BLOBS!

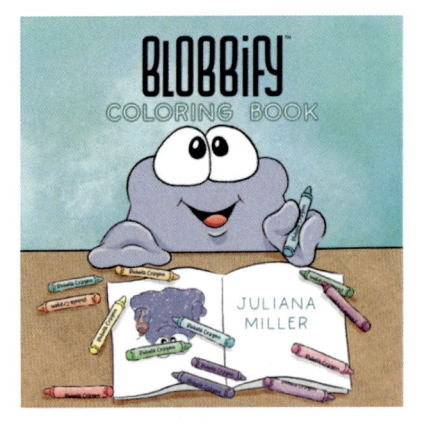

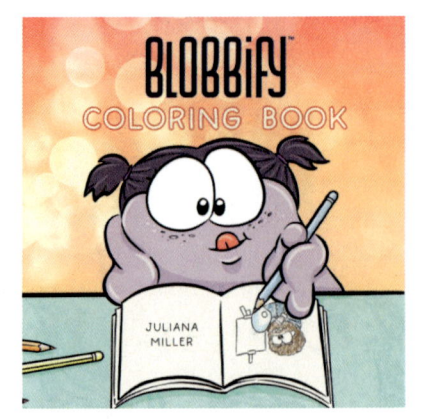

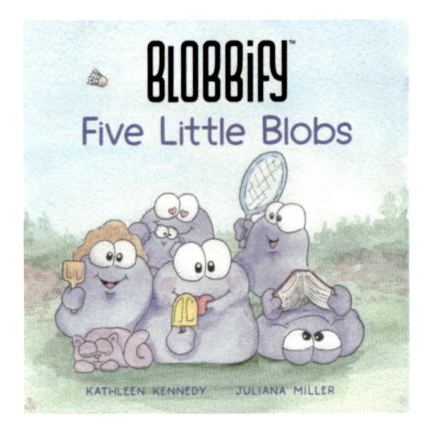

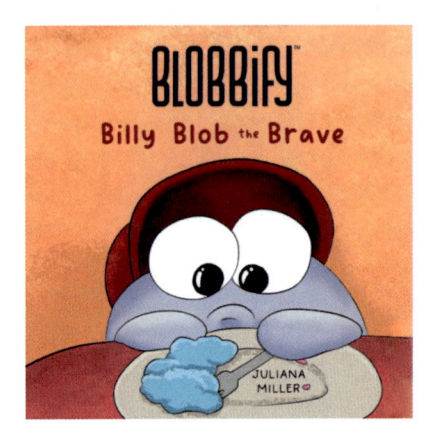

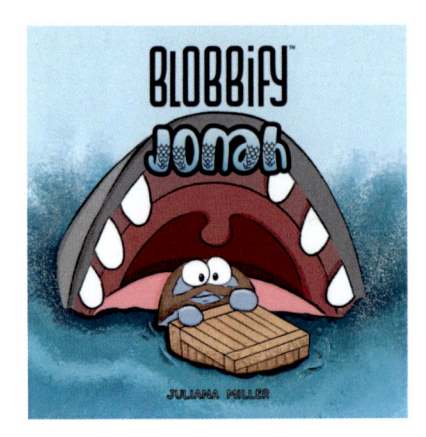

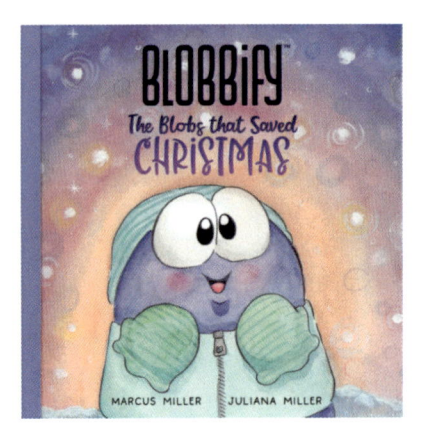

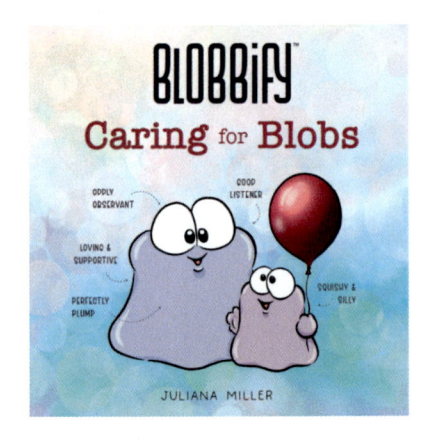

ARE YOU LOW ON VITAMIN B?

DISCOVER MORE BLOBS

WWW.BLOBBIFY.COM!

Made in the USA
Columbia, SC
05 May 2023